WOLF'S LADY

MAGIC & MECHANICALS BOOK 1

JESSICA MARTING

SHADOW PRESS

Wolf's Lady (Magic & Mechanicals Book 1)

Copyright © 2015, 2021 J.L. Turner

Second Edition

This book was previously published by Evernight Publishing.

ISBN 978-1-989780-06-0

Cover art by German Creative

This book is a work of fiction. Names, characters, places, and incidents are products of the author's imagination. Any resemblance to actual events, locales, or persons, living or dead, is entirely coincidental.

For BDT, whose love and encouragement will stay with me forever. I still miss you so much.

CHAPTER 1

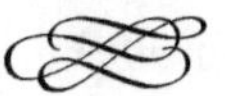

15 January 1887

*D*ear Lord MacAulay,

It is my understanding that you have received word from the Private Secretary to the Sovereign regarding your arranged marriage to my daughter, Lady Adelle Thornber. She will arrive at Roseheath with a traveling companion in the coming weeks and accepts that the barony is to be her new home. We will miss her in London, but all of us, including her, understand why this marriage and relocation is necessary. It is a suitable match for her, and she will run Roseheath Manor in the way I taught her, as a lady.

She is bright, but too strong-willed and stubborn for her own good. I wish you the best of luck in your marriage to her. You will need it.

Yours sincerely,
Lady Weatherstone

THE CHILL of the Scottish winter seeping into the carriage made Adelle aware that *it* was finally happening.

It wasn't the banishment from her family and London itself, nor was it packing her belongings for the forced journey ahead. It wasn't even seeing snowflakes whirling past the carriage windows like a zoetrope, or the sight of the man who called himself her chaperone seated across from her. No, it was the cold.

The realization made Adelle feel childish, and the rage that had been blooming the last four weeks nearly exploded from her. She wanted to scream and pound on the carriage walls and demand that her escort return her to the city so she could once again make a case for herself and force her family into forgiving her for something she shouldn't even be guilty of.

She didn't deserve this punishment.

Instead, her escort smirked at her from his seat on the other side of the carriage. His one good eye raked over her conservatively attired form for at least the hundredth time since they set out from the inn that morning, and the thousandth since they had begun their journey from the city. Adelle didn't have the faintest idea why the Duke of Wexfield wanted to tag along on this wretched journey, and she no longer cared. The one-eyed weasel could ogle her all he wanted as long as he kept his hands to himself. He made occasional lascivious remarks to her in between his coughing fits, but nothing more than that during the three-day trip from London.

Officially, Adelle was no longer in a position where being unchaperoned through such a long journey would be considered scandalous. But her parents still insisted on one and saw nothing amiss with Wexfield when he volunteered. Or maybe they did and hadn't cared. His lecherousness wasn't exactly a secret.

The duke's clockwork eye remained trained on her, gripping the skin of his face with tiny silver claws and moving almost in time with his working one.

Adelle didn't ask how he lost it, nor did she care. She rearranged her fur-trimmed travelling coat a little more snugly around her and glared at Wexfield.

"I don't see why we couldn't have traveled in a dirigible," she said sharply. Wexfield had a dirigible. It was painted black, his favorite color. He rarely failed to mention it in conversation.

Wexfield laughed, a mirthless bark. Adelle only raised an eyebrow in defiance.

I am still a lady, and you will treat me as such.

"Ladies of your status don't receive the luxury of dirigibles," Wexfield said lazily. "I'm surprised you would ask that." His clockwork eye whirred as his gaze shifted to her chest.

Adelle clutched at her coat. A lady could still be a fallen woman.

And, oh, but Adelle was aware of her status. Being sold off to marry some minor noble in the middle of nowhere made her that much more aware of what was going on. Her family—genteel poor, but with a good title and on amicable terms with the rest of gentry—felt shipping her off overseas was just a little *too* harsh a punishment, but sending her to the farthest corner of Great Britain to marry a stranger was not. She was still being sent away from civilization as she knew it.

Is it going to be this cold all the time? She wished she could order the carriage to stop and for that hateful Wexfield to bring her a blanket from the hold in the back, but she knew neither the duke nor the driver would allow that. Adelle was merely cargo.

"We'll be nearing your new home shortly," said

Wexfield, looking out the carriage window and assessing the landscape. It was open and wild, with nary a building to be seen, the polar opposite of London. It was dark outside, save for starlight.

Heavy snowflakes hit the carriage windows. A blizzard would come in soon. *Perfect, absolutely perfect.* Late January wasn't a miserable enough time of year as it was.

A quickening sense of dread filled her, unbuffered by the hot fury that stewed in her ever since Will's betrayal. *Her new home.* And a husband who she didn't want and likely wouldn't want her. He had to be just as angry at being roped into this marriage as she was. She briefly wondered what Wexfield would do if she started to scream out her frustrations as she wished to do.

Or if she just wordlessly screamed, pretending she was unloading her rage into the proverbial void. Even that would suffice for a few moments.

Instead, she calmly reined in her temper and asked coolly, "How much longer, do you think?"

Wexfield withdrew a silver watch from his coat pocket. "Very soon, I would expect." He leaned across the carriage, his knees nearly touching Adelle's. She moved away instinctively, shifting her legs to the side. "Adelle," he murmured.

Her skin crawled. She did not like the sound of her name on his tongue. "Lady Adelle," she corrected him.

"Lady Adelle," he grudgingly amended. His good eye narrowed slightly, and the clockwork one softly whirred. "I can offer you an opportunity out of this. You won't have to marry Roseheath."

Ah, yes, Lord Henry MacAulay, Baron of Roseheath. Her soon-to- be husband, forever and ever. Despite her misgivings at listening to the Duke, Adelle glared at him archly. "I won't?"

"You can return to the city and your family, if you wish. I'm offering you a proposition."

Rage bubbled through Adelle. She had been offered "propositions" by other men of their class since her scandal broke. "Go to hell," she hissed.

The duke leaned back and laughed. "Not *that* kind of proposition. I see you've learned your lesson from last time."

Her ire was further raised, but she didn't respond. If Adelle had any idea where she was, she would have demanded to be let out of the carriage to walk the rest of the way to Roseheath Manor, blizzard be damned.

"No, this is a different one," Wexfield said. "I'm not looking for a well-bred mistress like your former friends were."

Humiliation twanged through Adelle like a harp's plucked string at the accuracy of the duke's statement.

"I need a wife," he continued. "You know as well as I do that I don't have a prayer of finding an appropriate wife among our kind." He gestured to his clockwork eye and coughed deeply. When he finished, he continued, "You also know that *you* don't have a prayer at finding a husband among them, either. It could be a very convenient marriage for both of us."

Disgust curled through her belly. "No."

Wexfield was unperturbed. "Consider it, my lady. I'm still a young man. Forty-seven can hardly be considered old, and I need heirs."

Adelle thought she could see fear flicker in his good eye in the carriage's gathering darkness, but she didn't know why. Just as quickly, it was gone, replaced by his usual disdainful smirk.

"I *need* them," he said. "I do *not* want my wastrel of a nephew to inherit this title. Your marriage to me would mean you could re-enter society and return to your old life. Of course, we won't have the level of respectability the Thornbers enjoy, but we would still receive invitations to the right parties. I have funds." He gave an uncharacteristic shrug that came off as forced. "You're a lovely woman, I've always thought that."

Adelle glared at him. "Never."

Wexfield again leaned across the carriage and had the audacity to place a hand on her knee. "You don't have many options, Adelle. Do you really want to marry this man, sight unseen? He's only a baron, for God's sake."

Adelle slapped his hand away. "Don't touch me," she snapped, her voice rising.

Surprise crossed his face, followed by anger. "You shouldn't have done that."

"Or what? What can you do to me?"

She regretted it the instant the words flew from her mouth. He caught her face in his gloved hands, his iron grip squeezing her jaws so hard she thought he might break teeth. She squirmed, but to no avail. "I know *exactly* what kind of whore you are," he said in a low voice. Rage crackled between them. "The *queen* and her whole fucking court know what kind of whore you are. So does your family. No one gives one good goddamn what happens to you. I am asking you for the last time, will you consider my offer?" He released her jaw and pushed her back against her seat. Her head smacked against the carriage wall.

She would not be cowed by him. "I already have," she said. She damned the tremor in her voice and hoped Wexford didn't notice her hands shaking in her lap. "The answer is no."

But she couldn't help but wonder which would be worse: marrying a duke over twenty years her senior, or the unknown Baron of Roseheath? Marriage to Wexford would be certain hell; she had heard the whispers at social functions, had seen bruises on his mistresses. She could handle a cool, aloof husband, even one who had a mistress as long as she and her husband remained civil to one another. She would not knowingly enter a marriage with someone who would abuse her.

Wexfield was quiet for the rest of the journey, and Adelle kept her eyes on the snow swirling outside the carriage. The wind rattled the windows. Not for the first time, Adelle wondered how the coachman was faring in the cold. She wished she had been permitted the use of a steam- powered carriage instead of the horse-drawn one; it would have been faster. She was sore from jostling around for days.

The driver's thump from the front of the carriage told her they were approaching their destination. Adelle and Wexfield exchanged glares as the carriage began a steep ascent up a hill to Roseheath Manor. "This is your last chance," Wexfield warned.

"No."

"I will make it my life's mission to make you sorry for that."

Summoning every scrap of courage she could, Adelle faced him squarely. "I wish you the best of luck in that endeavor, Your Grace."

Their eyes locked on one another in a battle of wills. They were still staring at each other when the carriage came to a stop. Adelle was vaguely aware of the sound of the coachman letting himself out, and the carriage door opened. Her anger was temporarily mollified when she truly felt the cold. It rushed through her layers of skirts and bit into her bones, and she gasped.

The coachman looked none the worse for wear, and he held out his hand. "We're here, my lady," he said, and helped her out to the snowy ground. He pointed up at the manor where lights burned brightly in a few windows. "I believe they're expecting you."

Adelle certainly hoped that expectation came with a roaring fire in the hearth and something to eat.

Through the darkness, she could make out a hulking ruin of a great house, stones crumbling on one side. It was as far removed from the ostentatious glamor of London that it made her heart sink.

The massive front doors opened, and a figure came dashing out of them, dark against the bright light illuminating the house. Two others followed behind him. Footmen?

"My lady," he said as he approached the conveyance. "We were getting worried. We were expecting you this afternoon."

"The snow delayed us a wee bit, sir," said the coachman by way of apology.

Adelle was shoved aside as Wexfield pushed himself out of the carriage. "Who are you?" he demanded.

"Lord Henry MacAulay, Baron of Roseheath," he said.

Surprise at the far too casual way he presented himself had her temporarily rooted in place.

This was the baron Adelle had been shipped off to? A man who ran out to meet her in the cold and snow and introducing himself? Was this how life worked in Scotland?

She chanced a peek at Wexfield's murderous glare.

The Baron of Roseheath still couldn't possibly be worse than the duke.

"Let's get in out of the cold," the baron said before she could form a response. "Philip, John, get her things from the carriage," he ordered the men waiting behind him. He offered his arm to Adelle.

They hadn't been properly introduced, but nothing of

this ordeal had been proper. She curled her gloved hand against his offered arm.

"You must be Lady Adelle Thornber," he said.

She finally found her voice. "I am." She couldn't really see him through the darkness and swirling snow, but his voice didn't have the creak of old age, and the arm under her fingers was firm and muscled.

As if he could read her thoughts, he said, "I realize this is unusual."

"This whole situation is," she replied curtly.

He led her up the steps. "Be careful, they're not in the best repair. Yes, you're right. This *is* unusual."

At the top of the crumbling steps, she turned around to look back at the carriage. Wexfield was griping at the baron's footmen and complaining about the blizzard, as if that could be helped.

"My lady?" the baron said curiously. "If you would take a few more steps, we could be sitting before a fire shortly."

His voice had a rich cadence that lowered her defenses slightly. In the light pouring from the manor, she could see he wasn't much older than herself, and his dark eyes had a kind, concerned look in them. She nodded and followed him inside.

THE ENGLISHWOMAN SENT by the queen's secretary shook a few snowflakes off her hat and stripped off her gloves. Henry's housekeeper, Mrs. Tuplin, helped her out of her fur-lined coat and clucked her tongue at how cold the new mistress of the manor looked.

There wasn't a great deal of propriety to be had at Roseheath Manor: the servants, while fiercely loyal to

Henry, had always spoken their minds. Mrs. Tuplin wouldn't hesitate to tell anyone that she looked chilly or needed to put some meat on her bones, or Henry's personal favorite, "Don't be stupid. Light a fire." He knew this woman had come all the way from London and had spent considerable time in society. She had a lot to get used to.

Behind them, the doors opened again and the footmen and the carriage driver lugged in a pair of trunks. Behind them, the man with the clockwork eye was quietly cursing under his breath about "this godforsaken landscape." He stared at Mrs. Tuplin, who was shaking snow off the lady's coat, and cleared his throat.

"Be just a minute," Mrs. Tuplin said cheerfully. "The poor lass here is half-frozen to death. What were you thinking, letting her ride up here without at least a horse blanket to keep her warm?"

The man looked like he was ready to open his mouth and roar at her for her impertinence, but Henry smoothly said, "Give that coat to me, Mrs. Tuplin, and I'll lay it out in front of the fire. Help..." He looked at his betrothed and the man for his name.

"Frederick Stone, Duke of Wexfield," the one-eyed man snapped. He took in Roseheath Manor's foyer, with its outdated, unused sconces lining the walls, the paper stained black from long- ago torches. "Good God," he said in disgust. Through the duke's eyes, Henry saw the shabby, threadbare carpet, the dry fountain with its fat, stupid-looking cupid aiming an arrow at the ceiling, the footmen in their faded and mismatched livery.

Henry didn't care about the duke's first impression of his home; what mattered was his estate and the tenants running it. Roseheath Manor may be in a state of disrepair that this duke and his wife-to-be weren't accustomed to, but he would not be insulted. Before he could say anything in the manor's defense, Mrs. Tuplin did so. "What doesn't meet your fancy, Your Grace?"

The duke and Lady Adelle were clearly taken aback. "How dare you," the duke said, but Henry cut him off.

"That's enough," he said firmly. "Mrs. Tuplin, where is Bensfort this evening?" The butler's absence was unusual.

"He's still fighting off that chill, sir. I sent him to bed after supper with a tonic and told him to stay put. It wouldn't do if he made the new lady of the manor ill on her first night now, would it?"

No, it wouldn't. Bensfort must have put up a terrific fight against the housekeeper. He wouldn't be surprised if she had strapped him to the bed and forced the tonic down his throat.

"Understood. Can you prepare a room for His Grace, then? It's too horrible outside for him and his coachman to go back tonight."

"I am not staying here, Roseheath. My orders were to deliver the girl to you and be back on my way. I must get back to London as soon as possible." Wexfield's clockwork eye whirred as he narrowed his good one at Henry. The threatening effect the duke was probably aiming for was spoiled by a coughing spell.

"What about your coachman? He must be frozen to the bones," Mrs. Tuplin protested.

The coachman shrugged. His ruddy face betrayed no emotion.

"There's an inn not too far off where we'll spend the night," Wexfield said. "We passed it on the way here. We'll stay there."

The slight wasn't lost on Henry, but he nodded. He hadn't prepared for a guest, not that he wanted the man in his home, anyway.

The footmen hauled in more luggage belonging to Lady Adelle, along with an icy blast of air through the door. The duke glared at them, then the trunk. "If this were ordinary circumstances, I would stay," Wexfield said, casting a contemptuous glare the lady's way. "Well, if this were ordinary circumstances, she would be traveling with another lady. But it isn't," he said almost gleefully. "So there is no reason to be concerned about propriety. I'm sure you know all about her sad story, Roseheath. So, Adelle, I bid you *adieu*." In a low voice that still bounced off the foyer walls, he added, "My offer still stands."

The duke's use of her given name did not escape Henry. He saw the lady's nostrils constrict as if she smelled something bad. She didn't offer a word in reply.

Wexfield and the coachman quickly left Roseheath Manor, the doors slamming closed behind them. Adelle stared at them for a moment before she turned a neutral face to Henry.

"My lord," she said and nodded her head.

He waved it off. "That will be unnecessary. Please call me Henry." She outranked him until their marriage took place, but he'd only bothered with formality during his brief time in Edinburgh at university. He had never had much use for the nitpicky manners of London.

Her eyes widened a little at this informality in front of the help, but she didn't comment on it.

"We need to get something hot in you," Mrs. Tuplin said. She turned to the footmen and ordered the lady's trunks to be brought up to the rooms she had prepared for her. "Come with me," the housekeeper said. "I've set the table for you. I'm Mrs. Tuplin, since the baron forgot to introduce me. I'm the housekeeper and cook." She led Lady Adelle down a long corridor to the dining room, but not before tossing her head to glare at Henry. "We're not much for manners here, but the least the baron could have done was introduce me properly to the new lady of the manor."

Well, he and his new wife hadn't been introduced "properly" either. And if Lady Adelle thought she could rest on her laurels and order Mrs. Tuplin to polish silverware, she would be in for a rude surprise. Henry couldn't help but hide a small smile at that.

He realized he still held her coat in his hands and turned into a parlor off the foyer where a fire burned brightly. He carefully spread it out on a nearby chair, noting its high quality. He wouldn't be able to provide such things for her in the future.

Henry sighed and went to the dining room to meet the wife that was foisted upon him.

She was very pretty, Henry had to grant her that. Her dark, glossy hair was pinned up at the back of her head in a practical style suited for traveling. Her deep blue eyes took in the dining room, lit with a combination of gas lamps and a flameless clockwork illuminator of Henry's own design, without a hint of contempt, which surprised him. Instead, he saw curiosity in their depths, and he smelled something else over her lily of the valley scent. A little bit of fear, perhaps?

He took a seat beside her at the head of the table. The table could comfortably seat twenty, although Henry couldn't remember the last time Roseheath Manor had that number of guests.

Mrs. Tuplin bustled into the room, bearing a tray with a simple meal of stew and bread. "We were expecting you earlier," the housekeeper said. "I had a proper spread ready for you this afternoon."

"This is all right," Lady Adelle said quietly. "Thank you."

They both sat in silence as Mrs. Tuplin served them and disappeared back into the kitchen.

From another part of the manor, a clock chimed ten times. "I apologize that the barony's vicar isn't here, my lady," Henry said. "He waited until six o'clock for your arrival to marry us."

He saw her gulp. "I wasn't expecting that so soon."

He shrugged noncommittally. "Why not?"

"As Wexfield said, you probably already know my story," she said by way of explanation.

He knew only the barest details of her having an affair with someone she shouldn't have, but didn't press her on it. He was certain there was more to it than what his orders from the queen's secretary contained, or the cruel descriptions of her in the letters he received from her parents.

She stirred her soup without taking a bite. "Propriety isn't one of my concerns anymore," she said. "No one will care if I spend the night here still unmarried and unchaperoned."

"No one would care at all," Henry replied. "Roseheath is so far off the map that no one gives a damn what one person or another does."

She met his eyes, and the determination he saw reflected there would have impressed him if her presence had been wanted. Her full lips quivered with an unsaid retort.

Her mouth is gorgeous.

The thought zinged through his head, and he forced it away. He would *not* think about her that way. The advantage to being chained to a woman who didn't want him was that she would probably let him continue his life and work in peace. Though he couldn't help but wonder what a society belle would do in this frozen part of the country. There wasn't much in the way of amusements.

"What exactly do you want me to be, my lord?" Lady Adelle asked, a chill creeping back into her voice.

"If you're wondering, I didn't want this match any more than you did. I'm consenting to it because the queen ordered me to," Henry said. He had not appreciated receiving those letters from her secretary, and the threats to have his patents refused if he declined. Nor did he like the tone of the letters from Lady Weatherstone, Adelle's mother.

"As am I. But what do you want me to be?" She inched forward in her seat to listen. All the traces of her former fear were gone, and in its place, Henry could only smell her perfume, and beneath it, the warm scent of her skin. It was a little dizzying.

He hadn't expected she would smell good.

He paused before replying, giving himself a moment to collect his thoughts. "I expect you to stay out of my way," he said at last.

He realized he'd said the wrong thing even before she raised an eyebrow in response. "What I mean is, I work," he said. "The barony depends on my work. It has to continue unimpeded. You also have my word that I will never lay a finger on you, nor will I ever force you to bed."

Some of the stiffness left her shoulders when he said those words, and her expression softened a little. While he hadn't answered her question yet, he was still relieved to see her reaction.

"I need someone to oversee my household," he continued. "As you can see, Roseheath has seen better days. I would like the manor to be repaired as best as it can with our limited funds."

She nodded. "I see. Anything else?"

"I wish for us to be friends."

Lady Adelle cocked her head to the side. "Friends?" she said curiously.

"This arrangement isn't what either of us chose," Henry said. "But we must go ahead with it, and having a friend at one's side makes facing obstacles so much easier."

"I suppose I am an obstacle," she replied.

An unexpected thread of pity wound through him at the forlorn look in her eyes as she picked at her food. She nibbled another bite and set her spoon aside. Before he could retort that she wasn't an obstacle—it wasn't as if he knew that yet—she added, "I was an obstacle to my family's standing."

"Do you want to talk about it?"

"No, not yet."

Henry didn't press her. But there was one more thing he wanted to ask her about. "Why did Wexfield accompany you?" The duke's presence was strange, and Henry was relieved the man hadn't wanted to spend the night at the manor.

"He is a family friend and insisted on being my chaperone, and my parents agreed. I apologize for his rudeness," she said. "I would be lying if I said he wasn't usually like that, but he is. And worse." She looked away from him shyly, her eyes focusing on something behind Henry. "He offered to marry me. I don't know why."

Henry's heartbeat rattled in his chest at her confession. "And you still chose to come here."

"Wexfield's a monster," Adelle said. Her voice wavered a little.

So am I.

Henry nearly said as much, but he had the feeling Wexfield was a whole other kind of monster unto himself. He waited for Adelle to continue.

"He was very insistent," she said. "I'm surprised he

didn't stay here the night, if only to try to convince me to return to London with him. Or…" Her voice drifted off. "Something worse, I don't know." She gave him a smile that didn't reach her eyes. "I'm being silly."

The anger Henry had felt over her presence lifted, replaced with sympathy. She was terrified and trying to hide it: of him, of Wexfield, her parents. She truly had no choice in how her life played out, and he decided he would not bring up the topic of heirs just yet. There was time enough for that.

Least of all the necessity to explain that his heirs would be werewolves. He was not looking forward to that conversation.

"Listen to yourself," Henry said. "To the little voice in your head that tells you when you're in danger. Wexfield didn't strike me as a considerate man, but if he was rude to you, I couldn't allow him to stay, anyway."

"Rude," echoed Adelle. "That's one word to describe him." A more genuine smile bloomed on her face. "Thank you."

"What for?"

"For not being terrifying," she said.

You haven't seen me shift yet.

"For wanting to be friends," she continued. "I can work with that."

CHAPTER 2

*A*delle's rooms were presented to her by Mrs. Tuplin after her meal. "These once belonged to the baron's mother," she said cheerfully. "Of course, she's been gone now for almost twenty years. But everything's clean and just waiting for the new lady of the manor." She smiled hopefully.

Adelle took in the sight of her new bedroom, with its threadbare carpet and faded drapes. But it was clean and warm, thanks to the fire burning in the hearth. It had clearly been decorated with a feminine touch: lace doilies had been placed on the tiny tables spread through the room, and the paintings on the walls depicted summer garden scenes. An oversized wardrobe, its doors hanging slightly askew, was pushed against the wall. The bed's canopy and linens looked new, and a few flameless candles offered the room substantial light. Adelle could see that a lot of care had gone into the room, and the manor's house-keeper had been looking forward to her arrival.

The last thing she wanted was to appear ungrateful to

someone who wanted her presence at the manor. "It's love-ly," she said finally. "Thank you."

The housekeeper beamed. "It was my pleasure, my lady. If you'll allow me, I can help you settle in. May I?" She pointed to one of the trunks waiting in the middle of the room.

"It would be greatly appreciated."

She moved a few things from her trunks to the wardrobe while Mrs. Tuplin told her all about the manor, the barony, and its tenants, everything she had ever read about London. Occasionally, she asked Adelle about her old life, avoiding the topic of why she was in Roseheath to begin with.

"What should I know about the baron?" Adelle finally asked, interrupting her. "I've been told almost nothing about him, aside from his name and title."

Mrs. Tuplin sucked in a breath. "His favorite dinner is steak pie."

Adelle smiled. "Beyond that."

Wariness crept into the housekeeper's voice, and her expression shuttered. Her ever-present smile turned downward. "Well, what would you like to know?"

Mrs. Tuplin's shift in demeanor was swift, and Adelle hoped she wasn't about to marry a murderer.

"Am I marrying a cruel man? A drunkard?" Somehow, she doubted Mrs. Tuplin would shy away from such questions.

She was right, and the housekeeper visibly relaxed, the smile returning to her face. "Oh, Lord, no," she said, a little over-enthusiastically. "He is a kind man, and good to the people in the barony. He employs them, he sends for the doctor when someone needs help, he takes care of us. And he rarely drinks." She arched an eyebrow at Adelle.

"And if you're wanting to know if he has a mistress, the answer is no. That's information I would be privy to."

That was a happy piece of information Adelle hadn't known she wanted to hear until then. "You've been in his employ a long time, then?"

"Yes, me and Bensfort. Thirty-five years each, all told. Since before the baron was born. How old would you be, if you don't mind my asking?"

Adelle schooled her expression into one of neutrality at such a rude question. "Twenty-four."

The housekeeper looked surprised at that statement. Adelle had been on the shelf for years. "Oh, he's not yet thirty. Not too much of a hardship."

Remembering Wexfield's hideous proposal, she nodded. If things had gone differently, she truly wouldn't have minded marrying a man the duke's age if he had been kind and decent.

"And we're to be married tomorrow?" she asked. She knew the barony's preacher had come and gone already; she just wanted to know how long she would keep herself tied up in worried knots until the ceremony occurred.

"Reverend Paul will be here about eleven tomorrow morning to perform the ceremony. If I have to drag Bensfort out of bed bodily, he'll be there as a witness." She helped herself to the clothes in the trunk. "Is there anything you might like to wear? Something special?"

Adelle hadn't had the opportunity to order a bridal gown, of course. Ladies of her situation were not privy to such privileges.

"I hadn't," she said honestly.

Mrs. Tuplin scrutinized her clothing and peered at Adelle. "This blue one is lovely," she advised, running her fingers over the fabric of a dinner gown. "Beautiful color. We get flowers in that color when the weather's good. Of course, that's about the only flower that grows in abundance here. Those and the thistles."

Adelle nodded. She didn't really care either way, but the housekeeper had been kind so far. "Thank you. I think I'll wear that one."

"And I'll help you dress tomorrow morning." She busied herself with shaking out the dress and hanging it in the wardrobe. "May I get you a little more to eat, my lady? You didn't have much at dinner."

How much should she tell Mrs. Tuplin? Part of her yearned to throw herself at the kindly woman and weep until she couldn't breathe. She wasn't sure she was still frightened of Henry, now that they'd met, but she was of everything else ahead of her. She felt like she was trapped in a hedge maze, in the dark.

"I'm out of my element, I suppose," Adelle said.

"Oh, you are. Quite a change from London, I'd expect. Can I get you some tea, at least, and then we'll finish putting your clothes away?"

"Tea would be lovely. Thank you, Mrs. Tuplin."

The housekeeper didn't bob a curtsy before she left the bedroom, but Adelle didn't mind.

THERE WERE two things that altered Henry's morning routine today: first, Bensfort hadn't let himself into his bedroom to help dress Henry—something he always offered to do before a special occasion, and which Henry always declined—and he was getting married in a few hours.

He didn't bother with any special niceties today, instead dressing in his usual attire of trousers and shirt. As soon as the ceremony was completed, he planned to return to his workshop. His new flameless candle prototype was functioning, but last night during dinner he had noticed them flickering, confirming his suspicion that they weren't quite ready to go into production. A pity, because he really needed a final design to keep his tenants employed. The new steam-powered carriage engine was looking to be a potential success, but he still needed to train his mechanics on its assembly. And there were still so many bugs to be smoothed out yet.

Impulsively, he chose a waistcoat that was a few years out of fashion and a dark coat to complete his ensemble. Both had belonged to his late father, and as Roseheath had so few visitors and fewer invitations outside the barony, he hadn't seen fit to update his wardrobe. But hell, it was his wedding day.

Philip, one of the manor's two footmen, brought him breakfast in his room. "How is Bensfort this morning?" Henry asked.

"Mrs. Tuplin says he's on the mend, and come hell or high water, he's going to be present at the ceremony this morning," the footman said. He stammered, "Begging your pardon, sir."

"None needed, I'm used to Mrs. Tuplin." He helped himself to one of the housekeeper's scones. "How is my fiancée?"

"I haven't seen her yet. Mrs. Tuplin said she was going to help her this morning."

Henry nodded and excused him. He drank the coffee Philip brought him and smoked a cheroot after opening one of the windows. Mrs. Tuplin would give him hell if she detected a whiff of smoke inside, he thought ruefully. The dark, cold fireplace remained unlit; werewolves didn't need the extra heat. Unlike his wife-to-be, who arrived at her rooms with a fire roaring per his orders.

He flicked the remains of his cheroot out the window to land in the snow two floors below. After washing his hands and cleaning his teeth, he took a deep breath to calm the unexpected butterflies that insisted on taking up residence in his stomach and left his bedroom.

REVEREND PAUL, the barony's only clergyman, accepted a cup of tea offered by Mrs. Tuplin. He took a seat in the drawing room, on a sofa opposite Henry, and made small talk about Henry's inventions, the Browns' new baby, and when the miserable winter would finally end.

Henry dearly wished for a glass of something stronger than tea, but didn't dare help himself to anything, not while Reverend Paul was present. He was more nervous than he expected to be.

At half-past eleven, Reverend Paul cleared his throat and finally brought up the subject Henry knew the vicar had been dancing around. "Henry," he said, his voice low and serious.

As always in his conversations with the vicar, Henry didn't mind the familiar use of his name. "I know what I'm getting myself into, Father."

"I've known you since you were a child, and I know how you feel about London and your family's arrangements there. I'm surprised you would acknowledge this order when you've ignored others."

"I was able to talk my way out of establishing factories in the city by using logic," Henry replied. He'd been ordered to move his first factory from Roseheath to Glasgow and refused, the first time the MacAulays defied Westminster or the monarch. It was a fight Henry won only because he promised to start production in Glasgow when demand called for it, a promise he'd kept. "I didn't have a good enough reason to get out of this," he continued.

"You don't know the girl! Could you not marry someone else to get the queen's secretary off your back?"

Henry shook his head. "There's no one here for me to marry. The ladies my age are already engaged or married, and everyone else is too young."

Reverend Paul fixed him with a hard stare. "What about your companion in Edinburgh?"

Henry stilled at the thought of Amanda. "How did you know about her?"

"I'm privy to all the secrets in this barony, including the one the baron keeps about his widowed lady friend."

"I'm surprised you approved of that relationship."

"I'm not supposed to," Reverend Paul said. "But you already know her. Surely, she wouldn't mind becoming a baroness."

"Amanda isn't one to give up the freedom widowhood gives her," Henry said. "Nor have I spoken to her in years, not since I left university. And she doesn't know what I am."

No one outside the barony did, save a precious few in the queen's inner circle. Someday, Adelle would know, but Henry didn't want to think about that just yet.

"And what about the girl?" the vicar pressed. "Lady Adelle?"

Henry shrugged. "If she truly wants to, she can return to London. Whether society will take her back is another story, I believe."

But she'd wanted to be friends, he recalled. She was willing to stick it out in Roseheath, just to try it out, if their conversation over their late supper was to be believed.

The old vicar looked stricken. "And you're taking her as

a wife without knowing those sorts of details? Why London wouldn't want to welcome back one of their own?"

"I know it can't be too serious, Father. You know what society is like. A lady has one too many drinks at a party and she's shunned. It's utterly ridiculous."

"Things are changing rapidly in London, and not just with automation. Perhaps if I sent a telegram…"

"No," Henry said firmly. "It was made very clear to me that I don't have a choice in this matter. This marriage is happening."

"Are you sure you want to do this?"

"No, but at some point I have to consider heirs. I'm the last of the MacAulay line. I don't want the barony disappearing." There should have been a spare to his heir, but his mother died in childbirth, along with his baby brother.

Reverend Paul blanched. "You're going to have to tell her about… well, you know."

"I know." *Believe me, I know.* Henry didn't know how he was going to get to *that* topic of conversation. *Adelle, darling, stay out of my way. It's a full moon tonight.*

A sneeze in the corridor made Henry and Reverend Paul jump up. They heard a hoarse voice arguing with Mrs. Tuplin, and soon the housekeeper and Bensfort appeared in the doorway. The butler was pale, but upright.

"How are you feeling?" Henry immediately asked.

"Better, but *she*"—Bensfort pointed at Mrs. Tuplin —"won't stop pestering me. I'm feeling fine," he said, glaring at the housekeeper. "You know I wouldn't have missed the lad's wedding for the world." Henry would always be "the lad" despite holding a title for the last decade.

Henry heard a light, feminine shuffling of slippers over the corridor floor. "Come along," Mrs. Tuplin urged over her shoulder.

A vision swathed in yards of blue fabric glided into the room. Henry's mouth went dry. He had thought her pretty last night, but he hadn't anticipated what she would look like in the light of day. Her dark glossy hair was pinned back, revealing her slender neck. Her full lips were slightly pursed, as if she were about to ask a question.

Or offer a kiss.

Her deep blue gown was one of the evening variety, and he supposed she didn't have anything wedding-specific in her trunks. He wouldn't complain about that, though. The gown undoubtedly left some of her upper breasts on display, but a shawl in a matching shade of blue had been wrapped around her shoulders, and Henry found himself a little disappointed at that. He chided himself for the instant attraction he felt, particularly in the southern parts of his anatomy. He was only supposed to be doing this out of a forced duty to a country he didn't feel any loyalty to.

Their eyes met, and for a bare few seconds he wondered again what exactly she had done that had sentenced her to a lifetime of matrimony to him.

Reverend Paul greeted her warmly, and she nodded and bestowed a beautiful smile on the vicar. Henry felt a stab of envy, briefly wishing it was he she gave that look to, and tamped it down.

The ceremony was quick, and only Mrs. Tuplin shed a tear. When Reverend Paul announced them as man and wife, Henry turned to her, wondering what she expected him to do.

There was sadness in her eyes, but they were dry. She forced a small smile at him and her eyes dropped to his mouth. "You can kiss me," she said so quietly he almost didn't hear it.

He offered her the barest of nods and quickly lowered his head to brush her lips with his own.

His blood heated, his inner beast roared, and he had to force himself not to kiss her more deeply. He kept his eyes closed after breaking the brief contact, praying his irises hadn't changed.

Damn it, why did she have to be beautiful? This would only make their ordeal more difficult.

When he opened them, she was still smiling, and it still didn't reach her eyes. But she didn't appear to notice anything amiss.

Henry breathed a quick sigh of relief. There was time for him to explain yet.

CHAPTER 3

*A*delle tried to establish a new routine in the days following the wedding, mostly studying the manor's finances and exploring her new home. She only saw Henry at mealtimes. She couldn't help but feel a sense of rejection at this; misplaced, she knew, because they hadn't wanted to marry each other in the first place.

The short conversations they had over meals so far showed him to be an intelligent man, and he was, she had to admit to herself, attractive. He was tall, and in his shirt-sleeves she could see well-defined muscles in his arms. His curly dark blond hair was a little too long and stuck up around his head in tufts, making her want to smooth it out, and his dark eyes often fixed on her with an unexpected intensity. He wasn't as dignified and put together as the men in London were, and she found she liked that.

But he seemed to avoid her outside of meals. She privately wondered if he had a mistress after all, but before she dared to ask that question, Mrs. Tuplin cheerfully informed her he had a workshop that he spent all hours in, where he built all kinds of household objects.

A workshop.

Adelle didn't have a clue where it could be anywhere on the manor's property. He must be responsible for the flameless candles and steam-powered machine Mrs. Tuplin used to sweep the carpets. Her interest was piqued, but she didn't want to disturb him.

Ten days after her wedding, she wandered to the library in the east wing, the opposite side of the house where all the household activity occurred. While the east wing wasn't kept shut up and closed off from the rest of the house, like so many decrepit homes, its upkeep wasn't a priority. The rooms here were dusty, with the occasional grimy white cover thrown over a piece of furniture. She came across a music room housing a piano that was painfully out of tune, and unused bedrooms, a nursery joined to one of them. Forgotten toys were stacked around the nursery, and she couldn't keep a smile creeping from across her face at the thought of her husband playing as a little boy.

The library was her favorite room in the manor so far. The vaulted ceiling stretched two floors, with small balconies overlooking the expansive room. The shelves reached from floor to ceiling and were crammed with books, all decades old with weathered covers. The windows faced a bare garden and stretched the entire height of the room, and a pair of doors opened into a garden, its trees winter bare.

Adelle decided to ask Mrs. Tuplin to have this room cleaned. But not today. This afternoon she would enjoy sitting in the winter sunshine with a book in her lap, a break from her hours in the study making a list of everything that could be repaired before the spring. She took a seat on a dusty velvet-covered chair, a novel from one of the shelves in hand.

I should've thought to bring a cup of tea with me. Next time, perhaps.

She had met Will in the library at his family home during a party.

The memory popped into her mind, unbidden. She had kept Will out of mind since her arrival at Roseheath Manor, and remembering him now only irritated her. Will, with his sinful green eyes and mop of black hair and his tall, muscled body, built up from years of playing pugilist with his titled friends when no one was looking. He was the heir to one of the oldest dukedoms in Great Britain.

Adelle thought Will had loved her.

She dropped the book like it was on fire, and it landed with a muted thump in the layers of her skirts.

She would *not* think about Will and his betrayal. Her life was now in the furthest reaches of Scotland, and she didn't hate it. On the contrary, she was far more intrigued by her husband than she ever expected to be.

"Here you are."

The voice startled Adelle, and she shrieked. For a horrible moment she thought it was Will, that he had taken it in his head to pay a visit to Roseheath and watch her humiliation. Or, just as awful, the Duke of Wexfield.

It wasn't. When she turned her head, she saw Henry standing in the doorway, an amused expression on his face and oil streaked across his shirt. "Don't sneak up on me like that," she chided him. "You scared five years off my life."

It was a surprise to see him at this time of day, a welcome one.

Henry held a plate in his hand, and he sat down in the chair opposite her. He offered her one of Mrs. Tuplin's fruit tarts. "Mrs. Tuplin said you like it in here when you're not balancing the ledgers."

She accepted a tart from him. "Thank you, and the finances aren't as dire as I'd been led to believe." Roseheath wasn't wealthy, but it was also far from insolvency. The repairs and minor renovations that needed to be made were within the barony's budget.

"You're welcome." He stretched out his legs in front of him. "So, what do you think?" he asked, gesturing to the expansive room.

"I think it's lovely, and I'll ask Mrs. Tuplin to have this room aired out properly."

"This was my mother's favorite place in the house," Henry admitted.

Adelle didn't know how to respond to that. His voice had gone soft at the mention of his mother. "What happened to her?" she asked.

"She died trying to bring my brother into the world." His voice was tight, and she wished she hadn't asked.

"I'm sorry."

He shrugged it off, but she could still see the pain in his eyes. "It's not your fault. It wasn't intended to spoil the library for you. I'm glad someone's getting pleasure out of it." He smiled, trying to lighten the conversation.

Adelle was glad to do so. "I thought you would be in your workshop," she said.

"You know about that?"

She nodded.

"Mrs. Tuplin?" he guessed. Before she could reply, he continued. "Well, it's not a secret." He paused. "I'm sure you've guessed that the barony doesn't grow many crops here, so I keep a lot of tenants employed manufacturing some of my inventions."

"Mrs. Tuplin's pointed some of them out to me. They're remarkable," Adelle said enthusiastically. "Why haven't we seen your flameless candles in London yet?"

"I'm still working on those. They're not quite perfect. Yet," he quickly added.

Again, Adelle was unsure how to add to the conversation; the topics she was knowledgeable on didn't include clockwork mechanisms or steam power.

Henry continued. "I don't believe in sitting idly by while tenants toil away solely for my benefit. I can't afford to, anyway."

Adelle had surmised as much, but didn't add to it. She would be receiving some pin money as part of the marriage settlement, but she didn't know where she would use it.

"The barony's manufacturing is still profitable, however," he said with a grin, and The way his eyes lit up when he spoke of his home was striking. It was obvious he loved it, and she felt a tiny stab of guilt for being so reluctant to come here.

His dark eyes took in her face, studying her, and she felt a flush creep over her skin. She hadn't forgotten their brief kiss on their wedding day. It had been only the barest brushing of lips, but it sent butterflies to her stomach and heat curling through her lower belly, in a way that none other had. She wanted him to kiss her again.

Or she could kiss him. *Why not? We're married.*

Instead, he inched himself forward on his chair, so close their knees touched. He took one of her hands in his and ran his thumb along the back of hers. His gaze dropped from her face. "Adelle," he said quietly. "I told you before I would never force you to do anything you didn't want."

"Yes."

He paused, searching for the right words. "I know this isn't what you were expecting," he said carefully. "You're probably used to something much grander than I can give you. And I'm sure you know I wasn't happy about this marriage either. But I'd like for us to be friends."

He'd mentioned friendship the night Adelle arrived, but what she felt for Henry in that moment was far from platonic.

His touch sent a sizzle up her arm, radiating to the rest of her body. His hand was warm and gentle, with calluses on the fingertips that grazed her skin. Her breath caught. Who would have thought someone could be so affected by just a touch?

A fleeting image raced through her mind: Henry's hands all over her body, Henry kissing her neck and marking a path lower... Her face and body suffused with heat at the thought.

Her husband stared at her, snapping her out of her reverie. An odd look crossed his face, and for a mortifying second she thought he could read her mind. "Are you all right?" he asked. His thumb traced along her wrist, right over her racing pulse.

"Yes," she said breathlessly.

There was a feral look in his eyes, something Adelle had never seen before, and she swallowed nervously. For a second there he looked dangerous, and it had an oddly exciting effect. Like she was something to be devoured.

His head moved closer to her, and she closed her eyes in anticipation. She felt his lips graze her neck, right where her pulse beat a wild rhythm, and she couldn't keep a little cry from escaping her.

He raised his head. The wild look in his eyes was still there, but he still managed to look concerned. "Adelle?"

"It's all right," she whispered hoarsely. She bit her lip. "Do that again."

He growled low in his throat, sending another thrill through Adelle's body. He dipped his head back to her neck, feathering light kisses there before he scraped his teeth against her skin.

She gasped sharply, her back arching at the sensation. *More, more, I want more…*

Why wouldn't he kiss her mouth?

Henry abruptly pulled away and turned his head. "I'm sorry," he said gruffly. He stood up, taking the plate with him.

"Whatever for?" There was a heavy ache in her breasts, between her thighs, that demanded attention right now.

He finally turned to face her. His face was impassive, the animal look gone. "I shouldn't have done that," he said simply. "I apologize, Adelle."

Before she could get a word of protest out, he strode from the library.

~

HENRY RETURNED TO HIS WORKSHOP, his body shaking. He had come very close to losing it in the library.

What in God's name is wrong with me? The full moon's a couple of weeks away yet.

He suspected that the airs she had when she first arrived at the manor were a defense mechanism against the unknown. He might have done something similar if he was in her position and forced to relocate to London. If she truly hated being here, she would have been sending letters back to the city, or demanding to be taken to the nearest train station, a day's ride away in Edinburgh. She wouldn't be exploring the manor or taking up in the library with a book.

He removed a flameless candle from a shelf and began taking it apart again, his mind still wandering. Not for the first time, he wondered what she had done to warrant exile to Roseheath. He did have an idea of how things worked in that part of the country. She had been labelled as fallen, a label Henry and his father had both loathed. She probably had a dalliance with the wrong man and ended up bearing all the responsibility, or said the wrong thing to a society matron.

He knew very little about the Thornber family, besides that Elias Thornber was the fifth Duke of Weatherstone, the family money came from distilling, and that Adelle was his only child.

He removed the flameless candle's wick and cleansed it in a solution to remove its liquid coating. The candles' flickering was a distraction, and while Henry knew their use wouldn't be a lifetime's worth, he wanted them to work for as long as possible. They were so much safer than the traditional ones.

Had Adelle delivered an illegitimate child?

He dropped the candle at the thought. It landed on his worktable with a heavy thump, and he grabbed it before it could roll to the floor.

He wanted to march upstairs right now and demand that Adelle tell him what she had done to warrant exile. He strode to the doorway, the candle forgotten, and paused when his hand touched the doorknob. He thought about what he should say. *Adelle, did you have a child you were forced to abandon? What did you do? By the way, whatever you did can't possibly be as awful as what I am.*

He couldn't do that.

No, he needed to remember to act like a gentleman. His father and Bensfort taught him how to do that. He didn't just play the role of kind, beneficial baron who treated his tenants with respect. He *was* one. And even though she wasn't a tenant, she was his wife who he felt an insane attraction to. He wasn't sure he could hold on to his resolve to be friends with her, not when she could strike him dumb just by looking at him with those big blue eyes.

Resolve firmly in mind, he turned back to his worktable. That flameless candle needed to be further perfected, and he was almost done with the prosthetic limb he had been working on these last few weeks. It was supposed to be a surprise for a tenant's daughter, a little girl who had been born missing her left arm below the elbow. She would be ten years old in the spring, and he wanted it to be a birthday gift.

He unbuttoned his shirt at the throat and set back to work.

ADELLE SIGHED and turned the page of the ledger in front of her. She had a good head for numbers, something she hadn't known would be useful here. The barony had enough, something the people she grew up around hadn't had a concept of. Henry seemed content, if not downright happy, to go without luxuries to better the lives of his tenants.

But he avoided her even more since he sort of kissed her in the library days ago, only emerging from his workshop or the fields or wherever he hid himself for meals, and it was driving her to frustration.

She hadn't expected to feel this kind of frustration in this marriage and didn't like it.

She didn't know Henry very well yet, but she certainly desired him. She thought he might be interested as well, making it even more maddening. *We're married. I don't see what the problem is. There's no reason we can't enjoy each other's company.*

Mrs. Tuplin let herself into the study, banging open the door to announce her presence. Adelle set aside the ledger. "The baron wants to know if you would like to go for a ride," she announced.

Salacious images flooded her mind. "A ride?" she finally squeaked, feeling her face redden. It took her a few seconds to figure out what the housekeeper meant. "I mean, horseback riding?"

"Of course." Mrs. Tuplin obviously didn't realize what Adelle had been thinking of. "You know how to ride?"

Well, yes, but the kind of ride she was thinking of at that moment was the kind that got her into trouble to begin with. "I do," said Adelle, standing up and setting aside her pen.

Bundled up in heavy coats, Mrs. Tuplin led Adelle out of the house through a servants' door, the snow crunching under their boots. Adelle got her first good look at the manor's property since her arrival and noticed the house didn't look as terrifying in daylight as it did her first night. There was a building that looked like a greenhouse which explained where Mrs. Tuplin got some of her fresh vegetables this time of year. Brittle branches stripped of greenery outlined shrubbery, and a fountain that was a larger version of the unused one in the manor's foyer reached gracefully to the sky. They crossed over a snowy field and through a copse of trees, following a pair of footprints.

They led to a well-maintained stable. Mrs. Tuplin opened the door and gestured for Adelle to enter first. It was warmer in here, and she saw an odd potbellied stove that looked like it ran without fire. It emitted a low buzzing sound, and there was a crank on its side. Henry stood beside it, winding its handle. At the sight of Adelle, his face bloomed into a smile.

"Hello," she said, feeling a little awkward. Despite the

chill, he wasn't wearing a coat, only a threadbare jacket that had seen better days.

"You braved the cold and came out," he said, and the delight in his voice warmed her heart and other regions.

"You didn't think I would?"

"I didn't know what to think."

He and Adelle locked eyes for a moment, and she was only dimly aware of Mrs. Tuplin excusing herself and shuffling out of the stable.

"I hope you don't mind, but I took the liberty of picking out a horse for you," Henry said, leading her to a stall. There were six altogether, all occupied. He opened the door where a lovely brown horse snorted at their entrance. White spots dotted its flank and nose. It was already saddled, and Adelle led her out into the stall.

"What's his name?" she asked.

"Her. She's called Josie." He was leading his own animal out, one that was entirely black except for his white tail.

"She's beautiful. Thank you."

Henry shrugged into a heavy coat and gloves before they walked out of the stable. He closed the door behind them and helped Adelle onto the back of her horse before mounting his own. "Where are we going?" she asked.

"I thought I'd show you the estate and the village. I don't blame you for not wanting to leave the house yet. It's been too cold." Henry didn't look the least bit perturbed at the chill in the air as he walked his horse out of the stable. She followed him with Josie at her side.

"I wouldn't have known where to go anyway," Adelle admitted.

They rode in silence, Henry shooting her appreciative glances now and then. Adelle *did* know how to ride a horse.

They rode through a small wood bordering his property into the village proper. "You're in charge of all of this?" she asked, surveying the cottages. Smoke curled from the homes' chimneys, and some had clumsily built snowmen leaning against the walls. They passed a coppersmith pounding away at thin strips of metal in his shop in the open air, who lifted his hand in a wave at the sight of Henry and Adelle.

"All sixty-eight tenants," Henry confirmed. "This isn't the largest or fanciest barony, but we all know and respect one another. My—*our* household—continues to buy things like eggs and milk from the villagers rather than owning a farm and selling it to them. Farming doesn't fall into my talents, anyway.

"I don't believe that anyone has the right to be a despot simply because he was born into it," he continued. "We all depend on each other here."

He stopped his horse when a young woman jogged up to him, a pair of young boys in tow. Adelle followed suit. "My lord!" she said excitedly. "I don't mean to interrupt you, but is this your new wife?"

Henry's smile was warm. "Yes, this is Lady Adelle. She's been here just for a couple of weeks. It's finally warmed up enough for her to venture out. My lady, this is Mrs. Carter. She's the village dressmaker."

It was the first time she'd heard such formalities from her husband, save their first meeting when he met her, and she wasn't sure she liked it. She liked being just Adelle with him.

"How do you do," Adelle said. "I'm sure we'll be meeting again soon. I'll be looking for heavier dresses suitable for winter."

Mrs. Carter beamed. "Of course, my lady. Come by my house any time. Charlie! Jamie!" she called to a pair of children rolling snowballs. "Come meet the new baroness!"

One of the boys whipped a snowball at his brother, who pelted him back. Mrs. Carter stomped through the snow, chiding them. "I told you, stop that. Show some manners!" She took a mittened hand in each of hers and marched them to where Adelle and Henry waited. "Boys, what do you say?"

A sullen "hello" was the response.

Adelle bit back a grin. "It's nice to meet you," she said.

Mrs. Carter sighed and shook their arms a little. "The pleasure is ours," one of them muttered.

Adelle and Henry bid Mrs. Carter goodbye, with Adelle promising to make an appointment at her shop.

They made a few more stops around the small village, including the small factory that produced Henry's inventions. Adelle was pleased to see that the tenants appeared happy and healthy. Like Henry said, there was a great deal of respect all around.

The local church was led by the same vicar who married them, its exterior well-kept and clean. "Reverend Paul would like me to attend services more often," Henry said when he pointed out the structure.

"You're not very religious, then?"

He shook his head. "I acknowledge the parts of the faith that emphasize fair treatment of your fellow man and observe the holidays, but not much else, I'm afraid. I go to services once or twice a month."

"I was raised the same way. Reverend Paul seems to be a decent fellow."

"He is. He makes regular trips to Edinburgh to help the church there as well. He tells me stories of the goings-on." Henry's face darkened.

Adelle knew all too well the rising poverty in the cities, something her parents never cared about. There were members of the gentry who volunteered their time and resources to help the poor, a group of people whose numbers had increased since the introduction of automatons had replaced their jobs in factories. Adelle's parents couldn't be bothered with such charitable endeavors.

The church marked the end of the barony limits, and they turned their horses around to head back to the manor. "You said farming wasn't your focus but the tenants, but I don't see a significant agricultural presence here," she said.

Henry shrugged. "It's not large, but it exists," he said. "The tenants are responsible for that, and anything that can't be grown or made here is purchased from Edinburgh. I do take enough to feed my household in lieu of taxes and I buy the rest, but other than that, the barony is self-sufficient. My grandfather began running things this way when he inherited the title, and it's worked out very well for us."

So Henry shouldered the barony's taxes. She hadn't come across that in the ledgers yet. He was generous, Adelle had to admit.

When they returned to the stable, Henry dismounted his own horse before helping Adelle down. He didn't let go of her hand right away, instead tracing the shape of it through her gloves with his own for a moment. The same look he'd had when he sort of kissed her in the library returned to his face, like he couldn't decide if he should or shouldn't touch her.

He leaned toward her, and Adelle closed her eyes in anticipation.

But nothing happened. She opened them to see Henry's face only a couple inches from her own, his expression indecisive.

Before she could talk herself out of it, she kissed him quickly, a light brush of her lips against his.

Without letting go of her hand, Henry looked at her in surprise.

Had she horribly misjudged the situation?

He also said he wanted to be friends in the library that day, don't you remember?

She felt like an idiot, and worse than that, that she had violated his terms of the relationship.

But he surprised her when his mouth quirked up at the corners. Without saying a word, he led his horse into the stable, and Adelle followed.

Gracious, but it was warm in here. The odd stove gave off as much or more heat as a fireplace did, and after she removed her horse's saddle and began brushing her down, she found she had to take off her coat. "Is that one of your inventions?" she asked, pointing to the stove with her brush.

She was desperate for any conversation that would take away the sting of what just transpired outside.

"One of my first," he replied. He replaced his saddle on a rack hanging on the wall. "A fireplace isn't practical in a stable, and it's obviously cold in February." He turned the stove's handle a few times until steam issued from vents in the top. "This was the second prototype. They've been in production for four years now, sold all over Britain now."

Adelle's respect for him ticked up another notch.

Their horses returned to their stalls; Henry and Adelle regarded each other for a moment. He looked like he wanted to ask her something, and there were so many things that needed to be discussed.

He broke their eye contact. "You don't have to tell me now, but…"

Adelle knew what was coming. "You want to know why I was sent here," she said.

He nodded. "I haven't spent a great deal of time with you yet, but I don't get the impression you're a bad person who deserves to be exiled here."

"This isn't exile," she said quietly. "I like it here." As she said the words, she realized how true they were. There was still a great deal to get used to, but she liked not being under pressure from her parents and society, and having her opinions on how the household should be run respected. She hadn't expected the latter in particular.

"Even after your life in London?" Without waiting for an answer, he strode away and lifted the top off of a battered wooden trunk beside the stove. He poked around until he produced a pair of dented tin cups and a bottle of something amber-colored. "Drink?" he asked.

"Please. I don't often indulge," Adelle said. "But I think now is as good a time as any."

He poured short drinks into the cups and gestured to a bench against the wall. "Why don't you sit down?"

"Why do I feel like I'm on trial?" she asked, but she obliged. She arranged her skirt around her and accepted the cup. She took a sniff and tried not to gag.

"You're not." He sat down heavily, and Adelle became very aware of the few inches that separated them. "I don't understand this whole situation. You grew up in a good family—"

Adelle snorted. "A family with a good title, you mean."

His voice softened a little. "All right. You grew up in a family with a good title, with royal connections, and was ordered to marry someone who's probably the poorest baron in the country, in the most godforsaken part of Scotland. I was expecting someone difficult, and yet you've gotten on well with my staff and you've been kind to the tenants. You haven't complained about your new circumstances at all. You should be a duchess on a wealthy estate in the south. Why are you here, Adelle?"

She countered with her own question. "Why did you agree to marry me?"

"I didn't," he bit out. "It was an order from Westminster and the queen herself. Roseheath wasn't in a position to decline."

"No one is in a position to refuse a royal order," she said. "Although I don't understand why you were forced into marriage with a fallen woman."

"I hate that term," he said. "There's no such thing. Ladies don't fall without a good push."

With that statement, she found herself liking him even more.

"And as to my not refusing this marriage, I was informed that if I did, I would lose the rights to all of my existing patents and all applications denied for future ones," he said. "It would be a disaster for the barony." He took a sip of his drink. "Your turn."

She considered glossing over the truth, but truth had a way of coming out eventually, and she didn't want to lie to him. She wanted him to trust her. "It was my own fault," she said. "I used to think I deserved to be a duchess, which is why I ended up in the mess that I did."

"A love affair?" he guessed.

She felt her face redden. "I thought it was love, but it wasn't. Will promised me a lot of things. I should have known better as soon as he said we had to keep our courtship secret."

"Who was Will?" There was a low, dangerous quality to Henry's voice that scared her and thrilled her simultaneously, a note she never expected to hear from him.

"William Throckington, heir to Claremore and a whole host of other titles," she said. "I was so flattered at first when he began paying me attention. You know my family's old, but we were on our way to the poorhouse." Adelle focused on the rack of saddles ahead of her, the old shame flooding her senses. "My great-great-grandfather established the family distillery, and when he inherited the title, my father never really paid any attention to it. Before automation became widespread, he didn't have to care, either. He hired managers, and he took a tour of the distillery once in a while, and that was it.

"And when automation began, he fired everyone," she continued. "He hired an overseer of all the machines who would work for less money than his manager. Unfortunately, the overseer didn't have any experience in distilling. And the whole operation had been barely making money before then, but he hadn't noticed." She remembered how angry her father was when Adelle asked if she could look at the books, because she was the only person in the family with any sense when it came to numbers. She knew now that he was embarrassed about his inability to run a business.

Adelle soldiered on. "He might have recovered from that if he had just apologized to some of his former staff and hired them on again. But they refused to work for him. Two had taken positions at another distillery as automaton overseers for more than what Father was paying them, and two others left for America. And…" Her voice broke, and a tear slid down her cheek. "Father had a terrible gambling problem. *Has* a terrible gambling problem. We could have weathered out the automation and lived on the family treasury, but he had burned through that at card games. No one knew until my mother and I finally looked at the books. There was a lot of yelling and screaming when that happened, and then they both got angry at *me* for not doing more for the family."

"And what could you have done?" Henry asked.

"A woman of my station is expected to marry well. I'm twenty-four, Henry. I'm well past the age to be put on the shelf, and I'm their only child. Finding a husband was the least I could have done."

Henry snorted. "Men aren't expected to marry so young. I'm more relieved than ever to be living here. I wouldn't want to be leg- shackled to someone fresh out of the schoolroom."

Adelle momentarily forgot her distress. "You wouldn't?"

"A girl that young is still a child. She should be studying or learning a trade, not marrying someone a decade or two her senior and having children before she's fully grown. You've heard what's happening across the ocean?"

"About women attending medical school in Canada and the like? Yes," she said. "I offered to go there first, right after the scandal broke."

"And?"

She gave a watery sigh. "They actually laughed at me. My parents said that I would be completely useless there, a lady whose only skills are bookkeeping and reading 'non-developmental' literature. I said I could be a teacher at best, and they thought that was even more amusing."

"Adelle," said Henry gently. "Emigrating and starting a new life isn't easy at all. I'm sure you would be a marvelous teacher to young children, but the kind that they need..."

She cut him off. "I know. Finishing school education wouldn't be necessary."

"It wouldn't."

Adelle nodded. "I knew I wouldn't be a lady anymore if I went there, and I was all right with that." She smiled through her tears. "I'm tired of being a lady."

His eyes darkened at that, but he didn't offer a response.

Adelle returned to her original story. "My family was still invited to the right parties, and my parents managed to keep our finances secret for quite some time. We had to let a few staff go, and Mama and Father talked about quietly renting out the country estate to bring in more funds. But they just kept living as they usually did, and none of our friends were the wiser."

"How did you meet this Will?"

She shook her head. "Our fathers were friends. Will asked me to dance at a ball his parents held, he began quietly calling on me, and things… progressed."

"Calling on you?"

"He climbed up the trellises outside and met me in my bedroom," she said in a small voice.

Henry stared straight ahead. "I see."

"He said he was going to ask me to marry him. He just had to get permission from his father." Her last words were spoken in an ugly, mocking tone.

"And you believed him!"

"Yes!" Adelle sprang from the bench and glared at him. "You don't know what it's like. Being my age and unmarried. I *wanted* to be married. I wanted to have a husband and a family and home of my own, just a little bit of freedom. I was tired of all the rude comments from my mother and the people who were supposed to be my friends. I wanted love and passion! I wanted commitment, and I thought that was what Will was offering!" She felt like stamping her foot on the floor in frustration, but resisted the impulse.

"I just wanted my own life." Her voice broke, and tears slowly coursed down her cheeks. "I was such an idiot. He told his friends about us, and then it seemed like everyone in London knew every detail of what we'd done. My parents wanted me out of the city as quickly as possible and made some arrangements or blackmailed someone, I don't know which, to get rid of me, and now here I am."

He was quiet for a moment. Finally, he said, "You expected to find all of that in a gentry marriage?"

"I'd hoped for it." Adelle said. "And all this time I've been pestered by my parents and people who were supposed to be my friends about my inability to catch a man."

"We're not fish, you know. And not all men are interested in an overgrown child with a dowry."

"I don't have much of a dowry," she said. "You received it. You know what it was. Perhaps five hundred pounds?"

"Three hundred and fifty, actually."

She sat down again, taking the spot next to him on the bench. "Brilliant."

"You know that's yours, don't you? I have no need for it."

"I can have some winter clothes made with it," Adelle said, thinking of Mrs. Carter's skills.

But something else pricked at her. "I'm not an overgrown child," she said sulkily, ignoring that by her protesting the term, she probably was acting like one.

"I never said you were. And if the stories I've heard about London society are correct, I'm not surprised you didn't find a husband." He held up his hand when she opened her mouth to protest. "I mean that as a compliment. You're very bright, and plenty of men in your circle don't find that a desirable quality. They aren't interested in commitment, either. I'm not even going to touch upon the subjects of love and passion. What about your parents?"

Adelle set aside her cup between them and looked down at her hands, at the unadorned gold band on the left. "I suppose they share a disposition to overspending."

"That's not quite what I was thinking of."

"I don't think they love each other that much, no," she admitted.

"Society match?"

She nodded, remembering her parents, whom she doubted she would see much of in the coming years. "Father had a title. My mother is the daughter of an earl and had a massive fortune, and I already told you what Father did with it." She sighed. "As I understand it, it was a marriage of convenience."

"So, do you know no one who married for love?"

She shook her head. "No, I wanted something different."

"You've been reading too many novels."

"Possibly." Adelle didn't only read novels, but she didn't see the point in correcting him.

"What do you expect from this marriage?" he asked after a pause.

She folded her hands neatly in her lap, obscuring her wedding ring. "Like you said, friendship. Respect."

"I'll drink to that." He raised his cup in a toast, and she picked up hers. They clinked them together, and Adelle took a tentative sip before coughing.

"Ugh," she said. "What is this?"

"Something Bensfort's family brews. Potent, isn't it?"

That was the kindest word to describe the swill burning a hole in her stomach. "Yes," she squeaked through the tears in her eyes.

"It's horrible." Henry offered her a smile that made her breath catch, and he tossed back the rest of his. Bolstered by the sight, she did the same and coughed. He stood up and held out his hand to help her up. "I'm going back to the house."

"Why haven't you married before now?" she asked as they put their winter clothes back on. She tugged on her hat and gloves. Henry gave a final crank on the stove. It groaned in protest before more steam issued from its vents. "What are you doing that for?"

"To keep the horses warm." He held the door open for her and they walked out of the stable. The sky was darkening and the wind picking up. He offered her his arm, and they began the walk back to the manor.

"You didn't answer my question."

He looked straight ahead for a moment, as if forming an answer she would find satisfactory. "I didn't want to," he said.

"I know you don't worry too much about convention, but there must have been a girl…"

The muscles under her gloved hand tensed, and Adelle realized she had struck a nerve.

"No," he said shortly. "If you truly want to know, when I attended university I was friendly with a widow in Edinburgh, a few years older than I am, but we never had any intentions of marrying and we lost contact quite some time ago. While there are young ladies in the barony and the surrounding lands, including ones who could have possibly made a suitable wife, there wasn't one I was inclined to court."

The latter thought hadn't crossed Adelle's mind. "I'm sorry," she said in a small voice. "I didn't mean to pry."

He exhaled noisily. "No, don't be. God knows I've asked you the sorts of questions that would have sent another woman running back to the city. You had a right to know."

Their boots crunched over the snow, and flakes began a silent descent from the sky. "Are you angry about all of this?" she asked. "You were ordered into this, too."

"No, not anymore."

They passed the fountain and hedges, and Henry

opened the servants' door for her. Once inside, Bensfort quickly took away their coats, and they were once again alone.

"I'm going to be away next week," Henry said abruptly. "Thursday night into Friday morning."

"Where are you going?"

"Just into the village," he said. "I'm helping Reverend Paul with some restoration work at the church."

That seemed within Henry's character. "All right."

"I'm not an avid church-goer, but I believe in what he does."

Henry was so far removed from the men she had met back at home. He cared about his tenants. He was helping the vicar at the local church, for heaven's sake. How many people had she known in London who would do something like that?

None. Adelle's heart lifted a little.

CHAPTER 4

*O*nce he was safely ensconced in his workshop, Henry began to rethink his excuse for his absence next week as he took apart another flameless candle.

The full moon was on Thursday, and he did *not* want to be anywhere near his new wife when he changed.

Once again, he thought about how to bring up his problem without her running back to London to report his condition to her family and friends. It would spoil everything the MacAulays had worked for since striking their deal with Westminster and the royal family generations ago. Never mind that his was the only pack in Great Britain, if not Europe, and they kept to themselves, never causing a moment's trouble. The wolves and humans of Roseheath had worked hard to keep their secret.

She needed to know about his being a werewolf as soon as possible. MacAulay children were always wolves. But he was damned if he could figure out the best way to tell her.

She hadn't batted an eye at her baron husband going

to work overnight at a church. He winced as he remembered telling her the lie. Reverend Paul would have him by the ear if that ever got back to him.

He was already dreading possible questions from her about all the howls she would be hearing come next week. Henry didn't want her to feel afraid at Roseheath. He didn't want her to view him or the other wolves as aberrations, slights in the eyes of God and a far-away government that didn't care about any of the barony's citizens.

Already he could feel his beast within him, growling to be let out of its cage. If he wanted to, he could change at will right now to let out some aggression; an alpha werewolf could do that. But his wolf had never handled enclosed spaces well, and the last thing he needed right now was to destroy his workshop in a crazed panic. And going outside at this time of day, when the household was still awake, would be a disaster. Mrs. Tuplin wouldn't stand for a werewolf inside, either.

How was he ever going to tell Adelle about what he was?

The barony had a well-earned distrust of the south, of Adelle's people. War was waged over the werewolf pack some four hundred years back, a battle so bloody that modern historians scoffed at its brutality, if not its occurrence at all. The remaining wolves had fled to the northernmost reaches of Scotland and lived in heavy secrecy, relieved when the royal family began denying the existence of shapeshifters and other supernatural beings until they were relegated to the stuff of legends after a century or so.

It was easier to be different when one's existence, one's way of life, was a total secret.

The Roseheath wolves had been so successful at living in hiding that no one was the wiser when their little corner of the country was turned into a barony, led by Henry's great grandfather many times over. The title had stayed in the MacAulay family since then, but there weren't any heirs to the current baron for the first time. Once again, Henry was reminded that he had to produce one lest the barony fall back under the full control of someone who wasn't a werewolf, an event that must never happen.

He sighed and urged his inner wolf to calm down, reminded himself that Adelle was safe with him, and set back to work on the candle.

It didn't have to be such a horrible thing, producing an heir with Adelle. He doubted now, or tomorrow, would be the right time to bring that up, though. She had been treated shamefully by that pathetic excuse for a man and pushed aside by her parents when she needed them most.

There was also that awful duke who acted as chaperone for her trip to the barony. Henry hadn't liked the way Wexfield's single eye roved over her or his leers. What were her parents thinking, sending him along?

She deserved better. Someone better than the man she called Will, and better than Henry, too. She didn't ask to be married off to a werewolf. But at least Henry respected her.

He certainly wouldn't have a problem lusting after her. Hell, he already was.

An image of her on their wedding day sprang to mind, her in that blue dress and the shawl that didn't conceal as much as it was supposed to. In his mind's eye he saw her hesitant smile, smelled the powder she had used on her skin, and beneath it, the heady scent of her. He saw the pulse flutter in her throat, the simple diamond pendant she wore that moved in time to the rise and fall of her breasts.

He recalled how she smelled in the library, how her

pulse beat under her skin. He had been surprised by how she responded to his presence. Surprised and immediately aroused.

A fresh surge of lust roared through him, and the front of his trousers grew tight. Beads of sweat popped out on his forehead, and he gripped the edge of the worktable, trying to force himself to gain control over his emotions.

The woman of his fantasies was only a floor or two away, but there may as well have been an ocean between them.

He looked at the flameless candle lying in pieces on his worktable, knowing he wouldn't be able to concentrate on it as long as Adelle was on his mind.

Since making love to his wife—he snorted softly when the term crossed his mind—was out of the question at the moment, he checked to make sure the workshop door was locked. He unbuttoned his trousers and took himself in his hand, so hard it was almost painful. Funny, he usually didn't mind the celibate state he had more or less spent his adult life in, but as soon as Adelle made Roseheath her home, all he could do was remember that she tasted as good as she smelled.

An alpha wolf should have more control, he thought.

Usually he did.

A low growl tore from his throat. This wouldn't take long. He just needed to ease the pain and finally gain some relief.

The force of his climax left him shaking, sweat pouring in rivulets down his back. He tasted blood where his canines had elongated and nicked his tongue. His whole body felt like it was boneless and insubstantial, and he rested his head against the table, gasping for breath.

He had thought that taking things into his own hands

would help relieve the pressure and get some of the lust out of his system. He noted ruefully as he set about cleaning up that it didn't seem to have worked.

ADELLE DIDN'T SEE much of Henry over the following days, and when they did face each other at mealtimes, he was withdrawn and… caged, somehow. Like an animal about to strike. She could see he was trying to act as himself, occasionally cracking a joke with Bensfort and teasing Mrs. Tuplin, but there was something different about him, and that made her a little nervous to bring up her ideas for the house. Well, just one in particular.

Her exploration of the manor complete, she, Mrs. Tuplin, and Bensfort had sat down together a few times about opening up some unused rooms, in particular the ballroom. "You're not wanting to hold a ball, are you?" Mrs. Tuplin demanded bluntly.

The thought had crossed her mind, but not with the guests Mrs. Tuplin was probably thinking of. "I would like to hold a party for the barony," she said finally.

The housekeeper and butler exchanged glances. "It's never been done," the butler said finally.

"Why not? Henry and the tenants appear quite fond of one another. Everyone works so hard to keep the barony running. Why not show our appreciation?" Adelle smiled. "I think it would be lovely."

"I know the baron said you have run of the house," Bensfort said. "As the lady of the manor should."

"He likes the tenants, he really does," Mrs. Tuplin added, then hesitated and looked away for a few seconds.

Adelle's suspicion was immediately piqued. "What aren't you telling me about Henry?" she asked. "I know he likes and respects the barony's tenants. Is this a financial issue? If you think it is, I've looked over several years' worth of the barony's finances since I've arrived, and we can absolutely host a lovely party for them on a modest budget."

"I'm sure of everyone in Roseheath, you would be the person who could pull off such an event," said Bensfort.

"I don't want to host the kind of soiree one would find in London. Believe me, I mean it when I tell you I want to put on a nice evening for the tenants, with some good food and drink, and dancing." She gave them what she hoped was her most beatific smile. "I do love dancing." An idea that might explain their reluctance seized her. "Does Henry not know how to dance?"

Mrs. Tuplin nodded. "Yes. He spent some time in Edinburgh and learned some of that there. Not that there's much use for it here."

"But there could be," Adelle insisted. It would be a fun, another way for them to get to know one another, and an excuse to have him hold her. She fought back a shiver at the thought of his hands on her. "I can help with more than the planning. I can follow a recipe and I'm not a bad cook." She had to learn after her parents had to let the family cook go.

Another look passed between Mrs. Tuplin and Bensfort that Adelle couldn't read. Finally, Bensfort said, "The baron doesn't usually like to have too many guests about the house."

Adelle knew they were withholding something from her, and it was infuriating. Still, she hoped her expression didn't betray her frustration with them.

Henry's hiding something, too. She believed his story about his upcoming overnight visit to the church, but there was something else about it he wasn't telling her, either.

"Wait until after tomorrow to ask him about it," Bensfort advised.

She knew this was the closest she could get to an agreement from the staff. "All right," she said. "I concede. I'll wait to ask him."

But when she and Henry sat down for supper on Wednesday night, the first time she had seen him all day, Adelle didn't ask him about hosting a party. If it was possible, there was something even odder about her husband. His sandy hair was more mussed than usual and his eyes bloodshot in the light of the flameless candles. If she didn't know any better, she would have thought he had been drinking. But he didn't smell of spirits, nor did his hands shake the way Adelle's father's did when he imbibed too much.

"Are you all right?" she asked after they finished their first course in silence.

Henry had attacked the roasted chicken on his plate like an animal. No, not quite like an animal. He still held his utensils like a gentleman, but he had stabbed at the meat and bellowed to Mrs. Tuplin about the lack of rare beef on the menu this evening. The housekeeper hadn't offered a characteristic snippy retort, but calmly apologized.

Henry stared into the light of the candle. "I thought I'd fixed that problem," he said, ignoring her question. "It shouldn't flicker like that."

"Henry…"

"Yes!" he roared, and she jumped in her seat. "Mrs. Tuplin, more chicken, if there's any left." He pushed away his plate, its vegetables and potatoes untouched.

"I'm sorry, sir, but there isn't." Adelle had never heard the tart- tongued housekeeper call him "sir" in her weeks at the manor.

"Damn it!" He jumped to his feet and paced the length of the dining room. Heart pounding in her throat, Adelle quickly scraped her nearly untouched meat on his plate.

"Here," she said, her voice a little more snappish than she intended. "You can have mine."

He stared at her, eyes narrowed. Adelle refused to cower and stared right back. Henry took his seat again and tugged at the collar of his wrinkled shirt. He looked at his plate for a moment, as if gathering his thoughts.

"Adelle, I apologize," he muttered. "I'm not feeling very well right now."

"You should be apologizing to Mrs. Tuplin," she said curtly. "I'm your wife. I know what to expect." She chewed a mouthful of buttery peas and carrots.

"No," he said and his gaze met hers. His voice was back to its usual register, with none of the dangerous undertones that had kept Adelle jumping over the last couple of days. "You deserve more respect than that."

He was acting like an ass, but damned if that remark didn't make something flutter in her chest. She set aside her irritation with his behavior.

"Henry, are you ill?" she asked gently. "Is there a doctor I can send for? This isn't just about your candle, is it?"

"No, I'm not ill. I'll be fine in a couple of days." He paused, parsing his words. "It's the bloody candle. I can't get it to stop flickering."

Adelle wasn't sure she believed him, but it wasn't as though she had a great deal of experience with men who had work ethics, anyway. "Tallow candles flicker," she said, trying to sound nonchalant. "As long as the wick burns, or whatever it is you've put in your flameless ones, what does it matter?"

"It's important to me," he said gruffly. "That much flickering is unacceptable."

She helped herself to some untouched potatoes on his plate. He watched her as she ate them, a different sort of feral look in his eyes this time, and one that made her feel self-conscious. "What is it?" she asked.

"You have a very sensual way of eating."

Of everything he could've said, that was what she was least expecting. *What in God's name is he talking about?*

Adelle covered up her nervous laughter with a strange cough. "What an odd thing to say." The words sounded inane even to her ears.

"It's true." His fit over dinner forgotten, he touched her face. "The way your lips move—your mouth is gorgeous, has anyone told you that?—and here, your throat." His fingers drifted over the delicate skin of her neck. She shivered at the contact, hardly daring to hope he would continue.

He moved his chair a few inches closer and his hand travelled downwards, tracing the erratic beat of her pulse and her throat where she involuntarily swallowed. "You smell so good," he murmured. Her eyes slid closed and she felt his breath against her skin. Every nerve on edge, she let out a little cry when his lips touched her neck.

"Henry," she whispered. Her hands slid around his neck, and she opened her eyes long enough to see him staring at her. That intense, feral look was back, but it sent a thrill through her rather than fear. She felt desired for the first time since her affair with Will.

Except the man beside her wasn't offering false entreaties or declaring improbable love. His head was marking a slow path down her throat to her upper chest, exposed by an evening gown she had always been fond of.

He kissed the swell of one breast reverently and she held his head closer to her body in encouragement.

He moved forward until he was in danger of falling off the chair. His arms tightened around her waist and his head moved into the hollow between her breasts. She felt the warm, wet heat of his tongue exploring her skin, tasting her.

Adelle's whole body felt hot, and her limbs were reduced to jelly. She felt as if she had had too much champagne, but it wasn't alcohol, it was her husband, worshipping her body through her gown. "Henry," she whispered again, urgency in her voice.

"Mmm?" His tongue dipped under the neckline of her gown.

"Henry, we could go to my bedroom."

He lifted his head. His eyes were half-hooded, the pupils dilated. Once again, she was briefly struck by how much they resembled an animal's right now. "Bedroom?" he asked thickly.

"Yes."

The sound of her voice seemed to snap him out of his haze. "No," he said quietly.

The word had such an air of finality to it. "Why not?"

"It's not a good idea." He ran a hand through his disheveled hair.

Adelle felt very stupid and, damn it, still aroused. Her body ached with the need for him to touch her again. "How—Henry, we're *married.*"

"I know." He shifted his chair back to his place at the table and attacked the chicken on his plate. It was probably cold by now.

"Go to bed, Adelle," Henry said gently. "Or go to the library. It doesn't bother me either way. But I need to get out of here for a while."

Before she could reply, he stalked from the room.

~

HENRY QUICKLY RETREATED to his bedroom, locking the door behind him.

He lit an oil lamp and opened a window, grateful for the freezing winter air. He hoped the chill would dampen his libido a little, but it didn't. Instead, he lit a cheroot and willed his heart to slow its rapid beat.

He breathed deeply, the cheroot burning in his fingers, and thought about what was going to come tomorrow night. The freedom changing into his wolf form brought him. The snow beneath his paws and nose, hunting a rabbit or two. Running across the frozen fields and through the woods. And finally, the relief when the full moon was over, when he was back to himself. No more snappish, wild-eyed, and ill-mannered ruffian to yell at the help and paw his wife like an animal.

He longed to find her and tell her the truth, let her know what the risks were in being married to him. Not for the first time, he cursed his werewolf heritage and the nonsense that made up the gentry. He hated the whole class system. He hated that he and his pack had to live in hiding.

Henry wanted a proper courtship with Adelle, a proper marriage. She deserved as much. He longed for them to have a solid foundation as friends, so when the passion wore off, they still cared for one another.

Somehow, he doubted his passion for her would wear away after time.

Crossing the room, he dug around his wardrobe for the hidden compartment built into the back. Inside the small drawer, he found the journal his great-grandfather had kept. Like Henry, he had been a werewolf mated and married to a human.

He hadn't read the journal in some time, but tonight he settled by the light of the lamp and opened it. Its leather spine creaked a little in defiance, but his great-grandfather's words were still clear and hadn't faded after all this time.

He had written about the differences in mates and wives, writing how fortunate he was to have found both in the same woman. *A werewolf knows when he's found his mate,* Henry read. *There isn't anything definable to it, but he knows by his attachment to her, his attraction to her, the compulsion to mark her as his.*

Henry hadn't marked Adelle tonight, but wanted to. He had to leave her before he left a mate mark on her neck with his teeth.

Could Adelle be his mate? He had always scoffed at the notion of mates. It was for life, and while marriage was as well, at least legally, mating was a deeper bond, one he wasn't sure he wanted to undertake, if it was even scientifically possible.

Werewolves are real, too, he reminded himself. *Your whole species is scientifically possible. Why not mates?*

Damn it, he hated it when his own logic worked against him.

HENRY WAS GONE when Adelle left her room the next morning. The manor felt oddly empty without him, even though they rarely saw one another when he was home. There was something comforting in the knowledge he wasn't too far away, tooling around in his workshop or meeting with the tenants. He was doing one of those things, anyway. But she was still a little put out to know that her presence would be unwelcome at the church.

Even Mrs. Tuplin and Bensfort seemed off-kilter today without her husband's presence. He was the center of a lot of universes, Adelle mused. Today she was wandering about the small portrait gallery, a little miffed that her husband hadn't shown her the artwork contained therein. She knew the feeling was irrational, that it was a result of his rejecting her over supper, but being left out still rankled her in a way she hadn't expected.

She liked him. She enjoyed spending time with him, and was looking forward to doing that in a way that wasn't in the dining room, or the village, or in the barn. Just the two of them in her rooms, closed off to the world, exploring each other's bodies.

Focus. You're the lady of a manor with a gallery any respectable house in London would kill to possess.

The Roseheath title dated back hundreds of years, so there were dozens of portraits to see, most of them beautifully rendered in the styles of their day. Certainly not like the ostentatious displays she had been subjected to in the city, with stiff, unsmiling nobles in pompous dress forever captured in oils. The artwork here had been created with a passion Adelle hadn't seen in the homes of her former friends.

There was a remarkable similarity between Henry's ancestors and himself: the same dark eyes, sandy hair, and serious expressions. Sometimes they were painted with women, former ladies of the manor, and occasionally a massive, hulking wolf. Some of the earliest paintings were inscribed with the name *MacAmhlaidh*.

Adelle couldn't help but shiver a little at the sight of the wolves, their eyes staring straight at her. The artists had captured them too perfectly, and they gazed back at her with almost human intelligence.

Why wolves? There isn't a wolf to be found anywhere in Britain.

She would have to ask Henry about it. There had to be a logical reason why his family liked wolves enough to be painted with them through the ages.

Those eyes are staring into my soul.

She turned and hurried out of the portrait gallery.

THE STAINED glass windows of the church couldn't hide the snowstorm coming their way, and they shook in their panes against the wind. Henry and many of the wolves in his pack had settled in the pews, drinking coffee and tea Reverend Paul had thoughtfully prepared. The vicar wasn't at all concerned that he was in the presence of a couple dozen werewolves who were going to change very shortly and didn't take any notice of the men and women who all seemed a little on edge. Already a few pairs of eyes had begun to change, taking on an animalistic luminescence as their pupils shifted.

A few people had tried to ask Henry about Adelle but were quickly rebuffed when they saw how ill-tempered their alpha was and instead looked away in a show of deference. Henry knew he was unusually quiet this evening; ordinarily he would be the first person to crack a joke to defuse some tension in the air, but all he could think about was Adelle.

He liked her. He respected her. He desired her, to the point of distraction. It was an ideal way to begin a marriage, save for the problem that would begin very soon.

He tossed back the rest of his tea, wishing it was the poison Bensfort distilled. "That's it for me," he announced.

"I'm going out early." At the sound of everyone else rising to their feet, he paused and turned around. "You don't have to follow if you're not ready. I just want to get this over with sooner."

A few wolves followed anyway, but he ignored them as he started shucking off his clothes in the church vestibule, not bothering to fold them. He opened the heavy wooden door leading outside, grateful for the bone-deep chill that froze his skin. In a few minutes, that wouldn't matter anymore.

He could already feel the change beginning, and he welcomed it. He only made it a few feet away from the church before he doubled over in the snow. Spasms racked his body, but he had learned long ago not to fight them, to just breathe deeply and allow the transformation to occur.

The sound of muscles rippling and bones reshaping themselves didn't bother him, nor did the moans some-where behind him as a few others followed him in their transformations, less gracefully than he had. Once he shifted, Henry sniffed the air and let the animal within him take over. Roseheath's troubles were no longer a concern, and even Adelle ceased to worry him. His toes spread in the snow, testing it, and he picked a direction and took off in a hard, exhilarating run.

He didn't have a destination in mind and just needed to feel free for the few hours his wolf's side allowed him. He wasn't concerned with encountering humans at this time of night, as every tenant who wasn't a werewolf knew to stay indoors during the full moon. It had been decades since a human had been injured by a werewolf, even longer since someone had been eaten, but Henry, like his father and grandfather, took no chances with the barony's safety.

He caught the scent of a rabbit and tore off after it. Another wolf raced alongside him, even daring to swipe a paw at him, but a snarl from Henry had him scampering away. He was *not* sharing one of the few kills he could find this time of year. His keeping them for himself was the only selfishness he indulged in. His shoulder throbbed a little from the other wolf's scratch and knew it would leave a mark after he shifted back.

When he finished his meal, he left the other werewolves behind and meandered back in the direction of the manor. Even his wolf side knew it was a stupid thing to do, but he didn't care. The stable was latched tightly so he couldn't get in and eat a horse, so he didn't have any fears on that front. The scent of horseflesh had never appealed to his wolf's side, either.

While his senses were heightened in this state, he still shouldn't have been able to smell Adelle days after she walked to the stable, but he swore he could. Paws breaking through the thick crust of snow, he wandered the area between the stable and kitchen door. Her small footprints were still visible, and he sniffed at them.

He was still thinking like a human, and it rankled his wolf's side. It didn't *want* to think about Adelle, but Henry couldn't stop. His human side wanted to force himself to change again and go inside the house, go to her. Mark her and make her his mate, even if he wasn't sure he believed in such things. He'd known her only a few weeks. It didn't make sense.

Instead, he settled back on his haunches and gazed up at the windows on the second floor of the ramshackle manor. Adelle's bedroom drapes were pulled closed, but he knew she was there and could imagine her sleeping peacefully. A knot of regret twisted in his stomach upon thinking about her. He should be there now, twisted in the bedclothes with her.

Howls sounded behind him, and he stood up and

bared his teeth at the wolves who dared to bother him. Two pairs of startled eyes met his before they dropped away, and the wolves ran off in the direction of the church, stopping occasionally to howl at the moon. Anger overtook him—for the wolves, for himself, and for the woman who had been forced into Roseheath—and he took one last look at Adelle's window before sprinting after the other wolves, kicking up snow under his paws.

CHAPTER 5

The baying of wolves ripped Adelle out of a fitful sleep. Her breath caught, and for a terrifying moment she thought an animal had managed to find its way into the manor.

Another howl had her stepping out of bed and crossing the room to the window and pushing away a heavy drape. The full moon cast its light over the grounds, and her breath caught in her throat at the sight before her.

A trio of massive, hulking dogs skulked around the house, their shadows cast by moonlight highlighting their size.

No, not dogs. *Wolves.*

Adelle blinked, then pinched the inside of her wrist just to confirm that she wasn't dreaming.

Wolves in Scotland! How?

She'd never seen one outside of a zoo, and the pair of wolves on display were nowhere near the size of the trio in the snow.

The largest wolf snapped at the other two, who scampered off. It growled at their retreating bodies before taking off in the same direction, stopping to bay at the moon before it bolted away.

But their running away from the manor did nothing to quell her heart thundering in her chest. Wolves were supposed to be extinct in Scotland; they shouldn't exist anywhere in Great Britain. With shaking hands, she closed the drape and crawled back into her bed. She thought about Henry helping at the church tonight and prayed to a god she wasn't sure she believed in that he was all right.

Perhaps they weren't wolves, just... huge dogs, as she originally thought. A friend of her mother's kept English Mastiffs as pets, and those dogs were the largest and most powerful-looking canines she'd ever seen. But the animals she'd seen in the snow were far larger, and they hadn't had any of the physical characteristics she knew English Mastiffs to have.

But they did bear striking resemblances to the wolves she saw at the zoo.

A shiver crawled down her spine, and she knew she would have to ask Henry about the beasts in the morning.

At the thought of her husband, Adelle fiercely missed him, even though they hadn't yet spent a night together. Her face grew warm thinking about him, when she thought about the last time they were together.

What if Henry had already returned?

The notion cheered her. Slipping out of bed again, she slid a wrapper over her nightdress and left her bedroom.

She knew the baron's bedroom, adjoined to hers, was unoccupied. Why Henry chose to sleep on the other side of the manor, Adelle didn't know, nor had she asked. She assumed it was because he didn't want her to feel pushed too quickly into the physical requirement of marriage, although she doubted they would have any issues in that area once he stopped acting so oddly. She picked up a flameless candle and used its flickering light to guide her through the manor's dark corridors.

There were a few bedrooms on the other side of the manor, ones that long ago would have been used for guests. She tapped at the door. "Henry," she whispered urgently.

She didn't receive an answer. "Henry," she said, more loudly this time. She wasn't worried about anyone hearing her since the live-in staff roomed in the manor's south wing. She twisted the doorknob, which gave with a slight squeak.

"*Henry.*"

The flameless candle revealed a cold room that smelled faintly of old cheroot smoke. A large bed, still made up, stood empty in the middle of the room.

He wasn't here.

She hoped he wasn't anywhere near those wild dogs or wolves, whatever they were.

Disappointment and frustration washed over her, and she turned back to her bedroom.

ADELLE WOKE up out of sorts, but still forced a smile to her face when Mrs. Tuplin arrived with a tray bearing breakfast. "Sleep well?" the housekeeper asked.

"Well enough," Adelle replied, hoping that her tone wasn't as impolite as her answer might be construed. She picked up her teacup and took a sip, relishing its small heat. She crossed the room and opened the drape.

The morning was gray, and snow gently wafted to the ground. But there wasn't enough yet to fill in the paw prints that looped around the bare back garden.

I knew I wasn't dreaming!

"Did you hear anything last night?" Adelle asked.

Was it her imagination, or did Mrs. Tuplin blanch at the question? "What do you mean?" she asked, quickly recovering.

"I heard animals howling last night," Adelle replied. "I think they woke me up. They sounded like wolves."

Mrs. Tuplin shook her head and started making the bed. Her gaze didn't meet Adelle's. "Dogs, perhaps. There's a lot more wild animals here than what you're used to, I'm sure."

What was she hiding?

Not wanting to alienate Mrs. Tuplin, Adelle resolved to ask Henry about the wolves instead. She let the subject drop and started eating her breakfast instead.

After she washed up and dressed, she left her room in search of Henry. She found Bensfort at the foot of the stairs, examining the dry fountain. She was determined to maintain her composure and not take out her irritations this morning on the help. "Good morning, Bensfort," she said. "Has my husband returned home yet?"

"He was back earlier this morning," he said. "He went to sleep straight away."

"Thank you, Bensfort."

She turned around and marched back upstairs. She told herself she was just going to see that he was home and safe. She was not going to wake him up and demand a minute-by-minute recounting of everything that occurred last night, although she did want to know if he had seen those wild animals.

His bedroom door was unlocked, and she stole inside, closing it behind her. The room's drapes were closed, letting in only a bare sliver of light, and the fireplace was cold.

She looked around the darkened room and spied one of his flameless candles and switched it on. But what caught her attention was the man sleeping in the large bed. The bedclothes were pulled up loosely around his waist, revealing a naked torso and arms thickly corded with muscle. She knew all the work he did had to keep him fit, but he looked better undressed than she had imagined.

Should she wake him? She intended to before she let himself into his room, but seeing him looking peaceful and even innocent, in a way, made her change her mind.

Whatever he had done last night, it had worn him out.

She tiptoed closer to the bed. In the flickering light offered by the candle, she could see faint bruises and cuts decorating his arms, and she wondered what could have caused such marks. Without thinking further, she reached out to touch one.

Before she knew what was happening, she found herself tangled in a pile of skirts, held face down on the bed by the same pair of strong arms she admired just seconds before. A thread of panic gripped her when he didn't let go, just let out an inhuman snarl in lieu of words.

"Henry!" The pillows muffled her voice.

Immediately his grip on her relaxed, and she rolled over to face the startled expression of her husband. "Adelle," he said hoarsely. "What are you thinking, sneaking up on me like that?"

Any traces of the peacefully sleeping man he had been were erased. She realized she still held the flameless candle and dropped it on the bedclothes. "I thought I would see how my husband, who was gone all day and night, is faring," she said icily.

"You scared the hell out of me! I could have snapped your neck!" He ran a hand through his sleep-mussed hair and his eyes fastened on hers, almost pleading. "Don't ever do that again. Make a noise before you wake me up like that."

Her anticipation at seeing him again evaporated, and she forgot about how she'd missed him during the night, about the questions she had for him concerning the barony's wildlife. "I can see that you're well, aside from the injuries you sustained last night. I'll be on my way in that case." With as much dignity as she could muster, she shook out of her skirts as best as she could and moved to get out of the bed. Henry's arm around her waist stopped her.

"Stay," he murmured against her ear. His breath sent a shiver racing across her skin and her body heated, suddenly too constricted for her liking. "I missed you last night. I wanted to be here."

She wanted to offer a tart retort, but she was distracted when his tongue traced the shell of her ear. "Don't sneak up on me," he murmured. "I would love to wake up and see your face, but I don't care for surprises."

Speaking of surprises, Adelle decided to tell him about what she had seen during the night, before he could distract the thoughts out of her head. She hated to change the subject, but if he continued what he was doing, she would forget all about it. "Henry, I know this sounds mad, but are there wolves at Roseheath?"

He immediately stiffened and pulled away a little. The color drained from his face for a second, and Adelle knew she had hit a nerve. "I saw three last night," she continued. "Looking up at my window. I could have sworn one was looking right back at me."

"Are you sure you weren't dreaming?" he asked.

If Henry hadn't reacted the way he had, Adelle might have given that idea more credit. But Henry knew something was happening on the estate. "Yes, I'm sure," she said. "I know I saw a wolf, or at least a massive dog, and I heard howling last night. And there were paw prints in the snow this morning."

He ran a hand through his tousled hair, an unsure smile lighting up his face. "Roseheath does have a modest population of large dogs," he admitted. "They've been here for generations. I think they may have crossbred with wolves once."

That explanation would have made sense anywhere else but where they were. "There haven't been wolves in Britain for hundreds of years," she said.

"Not full wolves," Henry said. "Half-wolves, certainly."

"That's absolutely preposterous," Adelle said.

"It isn't," Henry insisted. "They don't bother us and we don't bother them. I've never been up close to them to tell for certain, but they're only wild dogs. All dogs are descended from wolves anyway." Henry leaned back against the pillows and pulled Adelle with him, her back against his chest. "As long as you stay inside at night, they won't bother you, I promise. It's a small population, and they've never harmed a soul in all the years they've been at Roseheath."

She turned around to face him. His eyes were hooded, and when she raised the candle, she saw how dilated his pupils were. A warm thrum of arousal pounded through her veins, gathering between her legs at the sight. Any other questions about the wild dogs fled from her mind. The sheet had slipped down in their tussle, revealing his bare hips, and her breath caught in her throat at the sight.

"Stay with me."

He kissed her with an urgency that quickly made her forget why she had come here in the first place, his tongue exploring her mouth as if it was his right. Right now all that mattered was this room and the naked man in the bed, who didn't seem to have any intention of letting her go.

Her hand slid down the muscled planes of his back,

under the bedclothes, to grip a backside that was just as firm as she suspected it would be.

She was losing her head.

She broke away from him and leaned her forehead against his to catch her breath. She needed to know what exactly he had been up to last night, and she couldn't ask him about that when he started unlacing the back of her dress. "What are you doing?" she asked.

"Would you prefer I stop?" His hands slid around the front to cup her breasts, then flick open the buttons there. Despite the layers of clothing between them, Adelle couldn't bite back a moan.

What had happened in the dining room was only a taste of what could be.

"No," she said, her voice a breathy whisper.

As both of them had pointed out in the days before, they were married. She could nag him about his whereabouts later. She helped him unfasten her dress and pushed it off her hips to the floor, not caring if it creased.

"You came to bed overdressed."

Adelle's hand traced down his chest, feeling the hard ridges of muscle there. It was odd for a man of the nobility to feel so strong, but she already knew he had to be on this estate. "I just wanted to see you," she lied, and the tiny, knowing smile that spread across his face told her he knew she was.

His fingers plucked at the front hooks of her corset, with enough clumsiness that Adelle knew he wasn't very experienced with women's garments. The knowledge offered an unexpected relief to her, since she wasn't very experienced, either.

He pushed away the sides of her corset and tugged at her combination, tearing the thin fabric. Before she could react, he sucked one stiff nipple into his mouth, and she moaned. Heat shot straight from his where his mouth tugged at her to her sex.

He released her breast and pulled her face down to his for a harsh, biting kiss that surprised her with its intensity. Without stopping, he pulled hard at the rest of her clothes, but the ripping sounds barely registered to her as he kicked away the sheets, pulling her flush against his bare skin.

She pulled away, just to see what he looked like, straddling his knees.

"Is something wrong?"

"Of course not," she said. "I just want to look at you." His eyebrow rose mischievously. "Like what you see?"

She pretended to peruse his gloriously naked body with appraising eyes. Strong, fit, and muscled, so unlike what she had been expecting when she was exiled to the barony. She ran an appreciative hand down his chest, past the hair arrowing down his hips, to caress his erection. He sucked in a harsh breath at her touch and his hips lifted toward her, urging her on.

"Adelle," he murmured. "My *God*…"

He hauled her up against his body, but before she could settle against his chest, he flipped her over to her back with remarkable speed, pinning her beneath him. He pressed a kiss where her neck met her shoulder, scraping his teeth against her skin in an oddly possessive gesture that made her heart race.

Her legs slid apart, and his hips cradled against hers. His arousal pressed against her thigh, hard and exciting, and anticipation raced through her in time with her pulse. She had never known such a feeling and hadn't it was possible. His hands loosely pinned her wrists against the pillows, fingers tracing the network of veins running under her skin.

"You're so fragile," he said quietly.

It was an odd choice of words, but it didn't pull Adelle out of her lust-addled haze. "No, I'm not," she assured him. She had never needed anything so badly in her life.

"I worry that I'll break you," he said. His lips found her neck and his teeth nipped her skin again.

"Henry, if you haven't noticed, I've been trying to convince you to touch me for days now," she said.

As soon as his surprise wore off, his gaze heated and he let go of her wrists to run his hand down her body, hooking one of her legs around his hips. His other hand explored the rest of her, sliding down her belly and plunging two fingers into her slick folds.

She arched into his hand, needing all of him. "Henry, please."

He withdrew his hand, and she felt him nudge at her entrance. He pushed inside her, and Adelle could have wept at the welcome invasion.

She felt very full and unexpectedly complete. Her eyes met his, and she thought she saw the same feelings reflected in his amber gaze.

Just as quickly, the look was gone, as his body withdrew from hers and pushed back in. She sucked back a greedy lungful of air, loving the feeling, and pulled her other leg up around his waist, letting him in deeper. He picked up speed, and she matched his thrusts as her hips lifted to meet his.

Her heels dug into his back and she bit her lip, only stopping when Henry pressed his mouth to hers. He held on to her wrists so hard she thought he might leave marks, but she didn't care. Already she felt the first stirrings of climax.

With a wail, her back arched off the bed. Explosions wracked her body, wringing her out, but Henry didn't stop.

His eyes shut tight and his pace increased, and Adelle could tell he was close, too.

With a strangled roar, he pulled out of her and stroked himself twice before spilling on the bedclothes. Finally, he sagged against her, his heavy weight sprawled over her comforting. For a few moments, they listened to one another breathe.

Adelle spoke first. "I—that was…" She tried again. "I don't think I could stand up right now if I tried." A giggle escaped her.

He licked her ear, making her squeal. "My God, that was good."

"Why did you…" She tried to pick out more sophisticated words for it, but failed. She might as well be blunt. "Why did you come on the bed?"

He rolled off her and pulled her against him. "I wasn't sure if you wanted to be pregnant yet," he said carefully.

Adelle hadn't been thinking that far ahead, but she saw the wisdom in that. "Oh." She felt him tense, then relax when she added, "It would be nice to have some time just for the two of us, I suppose. But children will have to come along some day." Even in the short time she had known Henry she had guessed he wouldn't expect her to be a broodmare, but both of them knew that having a family was important for the barony.

"Yes," he agreed, but it sounded forced. "Some day."

A few hours later, Henry washed, dressed, and slipped out of his room, letting Adelle sleep on. He couldn't keep a silly smile off his face as he made his way through the manor.

Mrs. Tuplin was the first to accost him in the corridor

leading to the kitchen. "Where have you been all morning?" she demanded.

"Sleeping off last night."

"It usually doesn't take until nearly noon for you to get over the changing," Mrs. Tuplin snapped tartly.

Henry was used to his housekeeper's insubordination, but he wasn't willing to go along with it today. She had been much more reserved this week, knowing he was on edge, and she had days' worth of observations and complaints saved up to tell him now. Still, the mention of what had happened last night had him looking behind his shoulder in case Adelle was nearby. *You're being ridiculous,* he told himself. *You would smell and hear her as soon as she stepped on the stairs.*

"I needed the rest," he said curtly. He was so tired he hadn't even woken up when Adelle let herself into his bedroom. "And please keep your voice down. My wife doesn't know about that yet."

"You haven't told her?" Mrs. Tuplin's eyes grew round.

"She hasn't run away from the manor screaming, has she?"

Mrs. Tuplin considered this, then looked up at the ceiling. "I know it's not my place, but…"

He had an idea of what she was going to say next and cut her off. "It isn't your place to be saying a great deal of the things you do, Mrs. Tuplin."

"It might be best to tell her sooner rather than later."

He refrained from snarling at her that he already knew that and nodded instead. "She's sleeping right now, and isn't to be disturbed," he said, sidestepping her statement.

Her eyes narrowed suspiciously. "How would you know that?"

"For God's sake, she's my wife." With that, he nodded, brushed past her, and let himself outside.

He saddled his horse in the stable, unable to escape the weight of Mrs. Tuplin's words or his own conscience. He had made a mess of his marriage already, and he couldn't even apologize to Adelle for it yet. He didn't have many whom he could turn to and ask for advice under the best of circumstances, and this was far from that.

Henry rode the short distance to the rectory. Reverend Paul was, as he expected, willing to speak to him. "It's always a pleasure to see you, Henry," the vicar said, not bothering with honorifics. "May I get you some tea?"

"Please. I appreciate that." Henry removed his coat and followed the vicar to his sitting room. "I've come to you to ask for advice."

"I assumed as much. I haven't seen you at services recently."

Henry winced. "Adelle and I will attend on Sunday," he promised.

Reverend Paul beamed at him. "I'm pleased to hear that. Now, am I correct in assuming that the baroness is the source for your visit today?"

He nodded. "She is."

"How are both of you taking to marriage?"

Henry paused, trying to put together a response that wouldn't offend the older man. They enjoyed talking with one another. They both enjoyed the marriage *bed*, but he suspected that wasn't what Reverend Paul was asking about. "We've become friends," he finally said.

"That is a positive way to begin an arranged marriage," Reverend Paul said encouragingly.

Henry considered this. "It's possible that this may work."

A furrow appeared between the vicar's bushy eyebrows. "You would not be here if this marriage was entirely happy, would you?"

Henry fumbled for words. "She doesn't know I'm a werewolf."

A clock hanging on the wall ticked away, marking off all the seconds the vicar didn't speak. "Honesty and trust are important to marriage," he finally said.

It was hardly the response Henry was looking for. "I know that."

"If you don't tell her, and she finds out on her own, she could very well return to London and petition for a divorce. This isn't just about your marriage, Henry. It's the entire barony."

Not for the first time, Henry's blood ran cold at the thought of the rest of the country learning about the existence of werewolves.

"I'm not sure she would do that," Henry said. "She was sent here because I was unmarried and Roseheath is as far away from London as she could get without boarding a ship. She was a ruined woman, if you'll pardon the expression, and forcing her into marriage with me was her punishment." Those last words left a bitter taste in his mouth. Adelle had not been ruined—there was no such thing—but she *had* been forced into coming to Roseheath.

If she did return to London, there wouldn't be anything or anyone left for her there. He doubted her family or friends wished to see her, and they could, if they truly wanted to. There hadn't been any letters from home for her since she arrived. Henry and Roseheath Manor was all she had, and the realization made him feel sad and guilty.

It was one thing to be saddled to an unwanted husband; quite another for said husband to be a shapeshifter. And a liar as well, he mused. She'd been completely correct in her assessing him and his fellow wolves as such.

"She wasn't ruined," Reverend Paul said, echoing his earlier thoughts.

"I know." Henry pinched the bridge of his nose, sighing in frustration. "How do I tell her about my being a werewolf?"

That was what he wanted most of all: someone to tell him what to do, to give him a good idea how to handle this.

The vicar paused, and Henry guessed the man didn't know how to broach the subject, either. Disappointment coursed through him.

Reverend Paul shifted in his seat, unable to meet Henry's eyes. "Have you… marked her as your mate?"

It was an intimate question, but Henry could answer it without any embarrassment. "No." He didn't add that there had been another opportunity that morning, but he'd resisted it. "I'm not sure I believe in mates, and anyway, I'd prefer to tell her about it before doing it. *If* I do it."

"Even if you don't attach any belief to mates, there are practical reasons for marking her," Reverend Paul.

"It's the equivalent of pissing on a tree to mark my territory." The words were out of his mouth before Henry could stop them. "I apologize, Reverend."

"It's all right, I've heard much worse. I'm not a werewolf, but I'm descended from and related to quite a few, and even I know that marking is an excellent form of protection."

"Against other wolves, and the ones here wouldn't touch her anyway." Henry was the alpha. No one in the Roseheath pack would have dared.

"For your relationship, as well. I'd be remiss in my duties as a clergyman to not remind you of the importance of emotional closeness in a marriage."

Henry had heard that, but he still wasn't sure he

believed it. While Adelle had turned out to not be the vain, empty-headed woman he had been led to expect, he didn't know if she would willingly wear a werewolf's bite mark on her neck.

"Tell her soon," Reverend Paul urged. "*You're* the alpha. You can change outside of the full moon. Maybe demonstrate that to show she hasn't married a madman."

"Just a wolfman."

"A man who turns into a wolf," Reverend Paul corrected. "But still a man. Tell her as soon as you can."

Henry already knew that, but he felt let down that the vicar didn't have a better idea as to how to go about it. "I will," he said solemnly, rising from his chair. "Thank you, Father."

He bid goodbye and returned outside to his horse. The cold usually didn't bother him, but this afternoon he couldn't help but notice it as the biting wind whistling in his ears.

ADELLE HUMMED as she dressed herself again, this time in her own bedroom. It was only her bedroom for now, she thought, tossing her ruined undergarments in the fireplace. They were beyond repair, and besides, she didn't want Mrs. Tuplin to be scandalized by the sight. As it was, she'd had to hurry, half-dressed, back to her bedroom from Henry's and hope no one saw her on the way.

She wasn't concerned that Henry had left her sleeping, as there was work to be done around the estate and she had her own waiting for her, as well. She found Mrs. Tuplin downstairs and consulted with her about the dinner menus for the next week, then asked her again about the practicality of opening up the ballroom.

The housekeeper stared at her as if she had grown a second head. Clearly she was hoping Adelle had forgotten her earlier suggestion of a party. "You've spoken to the baron?"

"Not yet, but I will." She had forgotten to do so this morning, but the day was still young. "Does no one in this barony enjoy having some fun? Yes, Mrs. Tuplin, I still want to host a party." Adelle could feel her excitement grow just at the idea of it. "Aren't weddings often celebrated?"

"In Roseheath, not on the scale you're speaking of, and not in the dead of winter."

"All I want to know is if it's possible." She pasted a smile on her face, hoping to convince Mrs. Tuplin to take her side on this. "I'll help with the preparation. I'll even start cleaning the ballroom."

"Dear God, no," snapped Mrs. Tuplin. Adelle's heart sank.

"I will not have the lady of the manor cleaning the ballroom herself," the housekeeper said. She arched an eyebrow, giving her a mischievous look. "And I don't want to work at this party of yours. I want to be dancing and drinking with the rest of the guests. I like Bensfort's whiskey."

That swill was supposed to be whiskey? Adelle remembered the brew she and Henry had shared in the barn, comparing it to the smooth whiskey produced at her father's failing distillery. But she smiled again, this time a genuine one. "Of course, and thank you."

You are a coward.

The words raced through Henry's head over and over

as he tinkered with a brass dust beetle. Rather than face Adelle upstairs and tell her the truth about who and *what* she was married to, he retreated instead to the sanctity of his workshop. The smooth stone walls were lined with sconces, now unused, and earlier prototypes of his flameless candles that sent uneasy light through the workshop. A pair of lamps burned brightly on his worktable, offering him plenty of light.

He liked her very much. *More* than liked her, if he was being honest with himself. He was in danger of falling in love with his wife, and the idea was terrifying.

In some ways, it would have been so much easier to have never married and let the barony die out.

He shook his head and pulled a spring out of the beetle with more force than necessary. Insect-shaped, it was the size of his palm and ran on a windup clockwork mechanism, designed to suck up dust along bookshelves and other tight spaces. Mrs. Tuplin was very fond of them, as were a few of the other ladies in the barony. The clockwork mechanism just didn't last long enough, only cleaning for eight minutes before needing to be wound again. It was almost as frustrating as those damned flameless candles.

If the line died out, Roseheath would be taken over by the English or the title handed to a sixteenth human cousin eight times removed that Henry didn't know about, and the entire pack would be in danger.

Clockwork cleaning machines weren't enough to save the barony from outsiders.

He had to tell Adelle, and even if she decided to leave and petition for a divorce, he would beg her not to reveal the secrets of the barony. As soon as possible. He would figure out the issue with heirs later.

Tonight, he resolved. After supper. They could share a glass of wine and he could explain what he was and offer her the choice to stay or leave. She deserved that, and he had to do that before his feelings further intensified for her.

Footfalls on the stairs had his ears pricking up, and he caught her familiar scent in the air. Before he could react, he heard a tentative knock on the wooden door leading to his workshop. Lust surged through him, mixed with anxiety. "Come in," he said. "It's unlocked."

Adelle pushed open the door. "Hello," she said shyly.

He stood up quickly, setting aside the candle. "Hello," he said, a catch in his voice. He couldn't help the effect she had on him, even when he was nervous.

"Mrs. Tuplin said this is where you work." She looked around at the stone walls and scarred wooden worktable and bench, at the tools and metal pieces littering the entire room. She slowly walked around the table, the lamps bringing an ethereal beauty to her face. Henry swallowed and tried to quell the pounding of his heart. She had that effect on him.

I wish more than anything that I was normal.

Her fingers grazed over a few tools, but she didn't touch the pieces of a candle scattered on the table. When she was this close, all Henry could think about was what they had done that morning, and how much he wanted to again. His gums itched as his canines fought to extend, one of the first signs of transforming into a wolf. Or it could be that his wolf just wanted to mark her. Neither scenario was good.

Adelle looked at him quizzically. "Is something wrong? You've hardly said anything."

He found his voice and croaked, "No."

"Am I bothering you? I can leave." She took a few steps back, but he grabbed her wrist.

"It's all right. You just surprised me, that's all. Even Mrs. Tuplin doesn't come down here."

She hesitated. "I wanted to ask you something," she said.

He prayed it wasn't about what she had seen last night. "Anything," he said, pleased his voice didn't waver.

"I'd like to host a ball," she announced.

He felt the air being sucked from his lungs. Whether it was because of relief or a whole other level of anxiety, he couldn't be sure. "You want to invite half of London to Roseheath?"

"Oh, no," she assured him. "I think I'm finished with London." She paused. "I *know* I'm finished with London. I want to do something for the tenants. They work so hard and they deserve a lovely evening, and we have that big ballroom moldering away here." She smiled. "Besides, I've always loved hosting a good party. What do you think?"

This just got worse and worse. While Henry loved and respected his pack, he didn't much care for large groups of people in his home. It was an unwelcome feature of his wolf's side and how territorial it could be.

But he didn't want to deny her, either. She already had given up so much for this life in Roseheath, and she hadn't asked for anything since her arrival.

He couldn't help his next words. "If that's what you want, darling," he said.

Her face lit up. "Thank you!" She stood up on tiptoes to kiss him, in a gesture that should have been sweet, but it inflamed all of Henry's senses, erased his mind of every-thing but her. He pulled her flush against him, erection pressing into her belly through her skirts.

Her breath hitched, and he pulled away to look at her. She looked even more beautiful in the light cast by his creations, dark hair shining and full lips parted. Her pupils had already dilated and her breath came in short pants. She was just as affected as he was.

He had a near-overwhelming urge to take her right there in his workshop and knew she would probably be amenable to the idea, but he stepped away. The last thing he wanted was copper wire poking them in awkward places, or accidentally rolling over glass.

"I'm not a muddle-headed girl who only thinks about balls," she continued.

Henry realized what she said before she did. As soon as she saw his face contort into laughter, she clapped her hand over her mouth. "That didn't help my case, did it?" she asked, her cheeks reddening.

"It was adorable."

"Let me try that again. I'm not a muddle-headed girl who only thinks about *parties*. Does that sound better?"

"I found the first one more entertaining."

"Of course you did." But she was smiling. "Henry, my point is that I'm not doing this simply because I want to forget my troubles for a few hours."

His chest constricted, all amusement gone. "What troubles?"

Did she know what he was?

No, he decided. *She would have run by now.*

Adelle tilted her head, looked up at him quizzically at his sudden change in tone. "None. I don't think I have any troubles, Henry." She looked at a lamp for a moment, but Henry suspected she didn't really see it. "I wasn't expecting to be happy here, but I am."

"I wasn't expecting you to be happy here, either."

"You weren't expecting to like me."

"No," he admitted. "I think we've both been pleasantly surprised by each other."

"Do you really think what we did this morning could be called 'pleasant'?" she asked, one dark eyebrow arching.

He scrubbed his hands over his face. "Stop looking at me like that! It makes me want to do things to you here!"

"Why don't you?"

He didn't bother trying to be discreet as he adjusted himself, hating that he had to do that in the first place. "Not here," he said. "It's not that I don't want to, but I don't want to break anything. You or any of these things."

"That's a good point." She instead looked at the collections of brass and copper parts lining a rickety set of shelves pushed against the stone wall, running her finger over some of them. "What's this?" She tapped at one of the clockwork cleaning machines he had been so irritated with earlier.

"I call it a dust beetle," he explained, winding one up for her. He let it crawl along the shelf, leaving a clean streak along the scarred wood in its path. "It's very useful for small spaces."

"It's fascinating," she said. She picked up another one and examined its brass underside.

"It has to be wound up more often than I'd like," he said. "I want it to last for at least ten minutes on a single windup before I put them into large-scale production."

"I saw something similar in London," Adelle said. "My friends' maids used them."

"Those are larger and only last for six minutes," he explained. "I wanted them to be this size to clean smaller spaces, and I've achieved that, it's just the timing I want to improve upon."

"How long do they last now?"

"Eight minutes. I'm almost there."

Adelle turned back to the worktable and pointed at the artificial arm lying in the middle, nearly finished ahead of schedule. "Who is that for?"

"The Ross girl," he said. "She's nearly ten. She was

born missing part of her arm. This is going be a gift for her." He shrugged. "Not as good as a real arm, of course, but it'll be better than the wooden one she's using now. More comfortable, too."

Adelle turned admiring eyes to him. "You really are incredible, Henry," she said softly. "I've never known someone who truly cares about others like you do."

He couldn't keep a surge of pride at bay at her words. "It's a joint effort. Appreciated people are happy. Which is one of the reasons I'm pleased you want to host a ball for them. Everyone enjoys a party."

"Except you," she said, her finger poking him in the chest.

"Perhaps I've never been to one with such a lovely hostess," he teased, clasping her hand and kissing it.

She beamed up at him. "Are you really all right with my hosting this?"

He nodded. He could handle having others in his home for a few hours if it made her happy. "I am." He lightly nipped at her earlobe and relished in her gasp. "Put your arms around my neck." She obliged, and he effortlessly lifted her off the floor, eliciting a squeak of delight from her.

"What are you doing?" she asked, holding tightly to him. He quickly ascended the stairs, her weight nearly nothing in his arms.

"I'm taking you somewhere I can have my way with you."

She snuggled into him. "Good."

He made it upstairs to his room as quickly as he could, arousal overriding his senses. But he couldn't silence the tiny voice inside that warned him to tell her about himself as soon as possible.

CHAPTER 6

The following days were a whirlwind of activity for Adelle, and she loved it. It felt good to be doing something… well, not *useful*, like Henry's work, but cleaning the long-disused ballroom over Mrs. Tuplin's protests, making it shine, and planning a party to host in it gave her a purpose. It was something to look forward to.

She spent her nights with Henry, making love and talking and making love again. She no longer lay about in bed in the mornings like she did in those long-ago days at her parents' home in London and early days at Roseheath. Instead, she was ready to face the day at the same early hour as Henry, dressing in her oldest garments to help clean the ballroom with the staff. Mrs. Tuplin lightly chided her for not knowing how to polish silver and taught her to do it, showing her where a king's ransom of spoons and knives were packed away in a dusty storage room, alongside stacks of intricately painted porcelain dishes.

Adelle learned the names of all the tenants' families from Bensfort and painstakingly wrote invitations to everyone, even those who the butler told her were nearly illiterate. It was important that everyone feel welcome and wanted at this ball.

Henry spent most of his days in his workshop or working with tenants as winter started to fade away. While snow and ice still covered the grounds and trees, now and then, Adelle spied a bird on a windowsill or branches sprouting green buds. Spring wouldn't arrive for a few weeks yet, but the cold no longer felt unending.

This afternoon, she planned to clean the ballroom's dusty draperies. The faded cloth was still serviceable, although she thought it might be better to switch them out for the slightly cleaner ones from the library. Still, she shook them out, deciding she would choose between them after she saw what they looked like when clean.

The ballroom's windows offered a view of the untended hedges outside the house, brown branches poking up through melting snow. When the ground began to shake and a grinding whine of an engine filled the air, Adelle ran for them. Snow flew in all directions as dirigible lowered itself to the ground, smashing the hedges.

Where is Henry?

She had to find her husband. He was somewhere in the village, and he must have heard the dirigible's noise.

She hadn't seen one since she before she left London. Without thinking, she ran for the ballroom doors that led to the gardens and dashed through them. Too late, she noticed the airship's black-painted hull, the favored color of the duke she never wanted to see again, and then spotted the duke himself descending a gangplank. Dressed to match the dirigible, his clockwork eye still unsettled her as much as it had the last time she saw it. He discreetly coughed into a black-gloved hand.

"Wexfield," she breathed. She thought she might be sick.

She took a few steps backward, aware of the cold still hanging in the air and very afraid of the man coming toward her. A growing crowd of tenants approached the dirigible, suspicion and concern written across their faces. "Henry!" she yelped, desperately looking for her husband.

The Duke of Wexfield halted half a foot from where she stood, so close to her she could smell the ever-present scent of pipe tobacco clinging to his clothes.

Dimly she was aware of snow seeping into her flimsy slippers, but she was too frightened to care. When she felt warm arms wrap around her, she screamed before she turned around to see Henry.

Wexfield didn't say a word, but an amused glint twinkled in one eye as he regarded the pair.

"What are you doing?" Henry snarled.

Wexfield finally spoke, his voice scratchy and dripping with irritation. "Obviously, I'm paying you a visit."

"What is the meaning of this?" Henry roared, letting go of Adelle. He lunged at Wexfield, but a pair of tenants held him back. The duke merely moved away a few inches, brushing imaginary lint off his coat.

"MacAulay, you're just so far away from civilization that you can't keep abreast with life in London," Wexfield said breezily. "Everyone who is anyone has a place to land a dirigible, if not his *own* dirigible. I've merely cleared some space for a landing site for you."

Adelle looked at the crushed shrubbery in dismay.

"Get away from here!" Henry roared. "Now. Away from Roseheath." He lunged for the duke again, but he was still held back by the tenants.

Adelle shrank back a little herself. She'd never seen her husband act in such a way, like he was ready to tear someone's heart out.

"MacAulay, you know as well as I do a duke outranks a

baron," Wexfield said. "If I want to land my dirigible on your sad tract of land, I will. I have those rights." His eye slithered over Adelle's form and she shuddered. One of the tenants who had kept Henry from ripping Wexfield limb from limb draped his coat around her shoulders.

"You do not!" Henry said. "I'll wire the queen herself if I have to, but you must leave at once, and take that *thing* with you!" He gestured to the hulking dirigible.

Wexfield sighed dramatically. "Actually, as much as I enjoy speaking to you, I came here to see your lovely wife, *Henry*."

"My wife wants nothing to do with you."

Wexfield turned to Adelle, one eyebrow raised. "Adelle?"

She straightened her shoulders. "I am the Baroness of Roseheath, and you will address me as such."

The duke's eye glinted with amusement, making her want to kick him. "How does one address a baroness? 'Your ladyship'? I can't remember, it's such a minor title. No, *Adelle*," he repeated, spitting out the word, "I came to see you."

"I don't want to see you. Leave, Wexfield. Now."

The duke looked at Henry and Adelle, and a grim smile stretched across his weathered face. "I see," he said. "This marriage has proven itself to be a love match, has it?"

Neither of them had voiced the words, but Adelle knew Wexfield's barb was for her. She loved Henry, and she would not let this self-important and cruel bastard take her away from him. She already knew that was what he wanted: to spirit her back to London and set her up as his mistress.

She refused to entertain that option when she was disowned, and she wouldn't now.

"You know she didn't want to be here, don't you?" he said to Henry. "You know what kind of whore you were forced into marrying?"

The grips of the tenants holding Henry had loosened enough so he could break free, and before Adelle could so much as scream, her husband neatly landed a blow on the duke's face. Wexfield stumbled back, surprise on his features, but didn't fall.

She moved forward, wet shoes and stockings squishing coldly between her toes, but a firm grip held her back. "Stay out of this," Mrs. Tuplin hoarsely whispered in his ear. "You'll only make things worse."

Henry punched Wexfield once more before the duke appeared to realize what was happening. He swung, but Henry ducked.

"They'll kill each other," Adelle said, trying to pull away.

The housekeeper's hold was surprisingly strong. "No, they won't. Your husband is much stronger than that one-eyed bastard, and he'll figure that out soon enough. Watch."

Already, the duke had stepped back and touched a swollen spot on his cheek that was already darkening. Henry panted, murder in his eyes, but this time he let the tenants hold him back. "Get away from here," he snarled again. "Never return. If I think my wife is in danger, I don't have any reservations about killing you."

"I will return," the duke said coolly, then winced. "Perhaps I'll bring my great-uncle's old rifle, the one he used when we were at war with Napoleon. It holds silver bullets very well." He smirked at Henry, then stopped when he noticed the stream of blood trickling down his nose. He whipped a handkerchief from a coat pocket and held it there, staunching the flow.

Adelle didn't have a clue what the duke was talking about, but when she looked at Henry, she saw the color had drained from his face. A few of the tenants wore the same expression.

Without another word, Wexfield retreated into his dirigible. A few seconds later, its engine roared to life, and it lifted off the ground, revealing just how badly the garden was damaged.

As soon as the dirigible was in the air and sailing away from Roseheath, Henry whirled around. "It's over, everyone," he said. "Go back to work. Adelle, Mrs. Tuplin, go back inside before you freeze to death." He stalked off in the direction of the village.

Adelle ran after him, shrugging off her borrowed coat in the process. The man who had loaned it to her walked alongside Henry and she pushed it in his hands. "Henry, come back to the house."

"Soon, Adelle."

"No, now." She grabbed his arm and dug her feet into the snow. He could have easily shaken her off, but he didn't.

"It can wait, sir," one of his companions said.

What could wait? What was her husband still keeping her in the dark about?

"We can manage the rest of the windows on Mrs. Chaplin's house just fine," the man added.

For an odd reason, relief coursed through Adelle at the thought that all Henry had been doing was helping to install new windows on a tenant's home. He was still keeping secrets from her, and she was determined to discover them, but he was still the kind baron dedicated to helping his tenants she thought him to be.

"All right," Henry said. He turned around wordlessly

and stalked back to the house, Adelle nearly running to keep up with him.

"Slow down," she said. "Henry, I know you're upset and so am I, but you're being an ass."

He stopped and faced her, regret written across his face. "You're right, Adelle. I'm sorry." Without another word, he picked her up and carried her to the house. It was the second time he had done this, and even though she was still reeling from Wexfield's unexpected visit, she still liked it.

"You don't have to do this." She protested, but she didn't pull away. She felt safe with him—loved and protected. Something she never experienced with anyone else, including her own family.

"I want to. You shouldn't be trampling around outside in this weather, anyway." Letting himself in through the garden doors, he set her down on the ballroom floor. "You're shivering," he said. "You'll catch cold if you do that again. You need to get out of those wet stockings."

Adelle kicked off her ruined shoes and ripped off her stockings. All were caked with mud and melted snow and were beyond saving; at least they were old and wouldn't be missed.

"What are you doing?" Henry asked.

"Obeying my husband." The alarm and fear she felt during Wexfield's visit evaporated. She was angry now, and she wanted Henry to tell her his secrets, why he had flinched when Wexfield mentioned silver bullets. It wasn't as if the man was a vampire. Henry and everyone else in the village could walk around in the sun. Henry ate with silver utensils every night.

Besides that, vampires didn't exist.

"That wasn't my intention, Adelle. I'm sorry." He

shucked off his boots as well, and barefoot, they stalked through the house to her—*their*—bedroom.

Once there, Adelle tossed her stockings in the fireplace and dug through her wardrobe until she found another pair. "I want you to know that I don't have a clue as to why Wexfield appeared today," she said. Pushing handfuls of her skirts aside, she struggled a little as she pulled on the first stocking, one that had been darned many times but was still serviceable. "I'd hoped never to see him again after he escorted me here."

"I know," Henry said. "And I'm not angry with you. He took me by surprise and insulted you. If you hadn't been there, I probably would have killed him."

His voice was now calm, but Adelle heard the threat under it.

Her husband really had wanted to kill the man.

"I don't understand his obsession with you," Henry continued.

"Nor do I. No one else from my old life has tried to contact me, except for this visit." Not even Adelle's parents had sent along so much as a letter or telegram. "I've rejected him so many times, and yet he keeps trying. And besides, you heard him out there." She barked a short, bitter laugh. "I'm just a whore."

"No." In two quick strides, Henry moved from the wardrobe to the bed where Adelle sat, stocking in hand. Tears pricked at her eyes, but she brushed them away impatiently. "I've never thought that, not once. Even before I received the order from London and the letter telling me who you were, I didn't believe it."

"Why did you *really* agree to this marriage?" she asked in a small voice.

~

Henry steeled himself. If he had summoned up his courage days ago and told her what he was, she might understand now that he had needed a wife for practical reasons, that there were so few available women. There was also the ever-present threat of the werewolf pack being exposed and hunted down again. "I needed to keep my patents, and I needed a wife," he said simply. "You know that. And a baron isn't in a position where he can reject an order from the queen."

"There was also my dowry," she said. The sadness in her voice tore at him, and it still hadn't stopped horrifying him that she had been a commodity to her family and that awful duke back in London.

Her worth wasn't comparable to mere money.

"It wasn't for your dowry." As he told her so many weeks ago in the barn, her dowry was too small to make a great deal of difference in the barony's finances anyway, and besides, it was hers alone. "We both know the nobility is expected to marry, and I need an heir if I don't want the Roseheath pack lands to be out of my family's control."

"What do you mean, *pack*?" she asked.

Too late, he saw his error. "Just an old expression," he lied, and mentally kicked himself again.

He was slipping. He was letting his guard down around his wife.

He was sick of lying to her, but he didn't know how to tell her the truth without her leaving him.

You're a horrible bastard, and you don't deserve her. He hated himself a little more every time he couldn't bring himself to tell her he was a werewolf.

"Old Gaelic expression?" she asked.

"Yes, I think so," he said. "My Gaelic is lacking, though, as my family rarely spoke it when I was growing up and I didn't finish my university studies. I'm afraid I'm a gentleman in title only."

That answer seemed to mollify her. She brushed away the last of her tears and unrolled the stocking in her hand. "Education and title aren't the only things that make a gentleman."

He relaxed a little. "Here, let me help you with that." Without waiting for an answer, he took the stocking from her hand and sat down on the floor, unrolling it on her foot.

"I did poorly in finishing school," she admitted. "My instructors said I was too easily distracted. I'm a very good dancer, though, and I can host a lovely party. You'll see at the ball."

He could hardly think about the ball now. If he could just bring himself to tell her about his being a werewolf… but when he tried to, he couldn't form the words. Her smooth leg was too distracting.

Desire coursed through his veins at the feel of her leg under his hand, only to be quashed with her next question.

"What do you suppose Wexfield meant with the remark about silver bullets?"

Henry swallowed against the knot of fear that bloomed in his throat. "I don't know."

"Silver bullets would be just as lethal as regular ones."

That bastard Wexfield was telling Henry he knew what he was, and he was threatening to expose them. Silver didn't affect wolves, but it was a popular myth.

It wasn't just the widow Chaplin's windows he had to attend to now. He and the rest of the pack were to figure out what to do about Wexfield, including the probability of having to kill the man. It wouldn't just be for Adelle, it would be for all of Roseheath.

Westminster, the royal family, and the Roseheath pack

had made a pact hundreds of years ago, and the pack had kept their word. If a duke decided to go against a royal order and threaten them, Henry and the rest of the wolves had the right to destroy him. He had never killed a man, but if he had to, he could.

He finally found his voice. "Adelle, I believe the duke is mad. That's the only reason I can think of to explain it."

Why was he saying that? Why couldn't he make himself tell her the truth?

Tell her! his mind screamed. *Tell her what you are!* "I promise you this, darling," he said, taking her face in his hands. "If he comes here again, I will kill him."

Her eyes widened, but she nodded.

"He means you harm. He's obsessed with you and your rejections have made it worse." She opened her mouth to speak, but he continued. "You were right to do so. I promise to keep you safe."

As he gathered her in his arms, guilt pulsed through him. Sooner or later, what he had been keeping from her would come out, and when it did, he only prayed she could forgive him.

It had taken days of hard work, but Adelle was pleased as she surveyed the ballroom. The ball didn't resemble the over-the-top affairs of her youth in London, but the atmosphere was still warm and friendly. Roseheath's tenants had dressed in their finery, occasionally dancing to the music provided by an increasingly inebriated pianist and piper, and partaking of the provided food and drink. They were enjoying themselves, and no one was concerned with following the strict social rules imposed at London functions. It was refreshing to experience.

Her husband cut a heart-stopping figure as well. She didn't know where he had found the coat or when he had the time to have it made over into the fashionable piece he wore now, but she knew he had done it for her. The poor man still thought she wanted to run back to London, no matter how many times she told him otherwise. He'd even cut his hair, and her hands itched to run through it, muss it up a little.

She still hadn't told him she loved him. The last time she told someone she loved him, the affair ended with her being made a laughingstock. She hadn't loved Will, and she knew that now. She wondered how he would react if she sent him a letter thanking him for causing her ostracism, because it made her happier than she had ever been.

Her relationship with Henry felt like a fairy tale, and she didn't want it to end. If he didn't love her back, she didn't want to know.

Henry took his place by her side, affection and something else in his eyes. Adelle's body prickled when he raked his gaze over her, his fingers grazing over her neck, sparking desire in a race through her veins.

This was *not* an appropriate time to feel aroused. "You smell good," he murmured against her hair. That wasn't helping.

His hand hadn't left her neck, an odd place for it to be, but she didn't mind. More than anything, it made her want to run off with him to another room and let him have his way with her.

As if he could read her thoughts, he breathed deeply and whispered, "Would you be averse to stepping away from the festivities for a few minutes? I don't think anyone would notice."

She gave him a sly smile and nodded.

They slipped from the ballroom without anyone noticing, and Henry picked up one of the flameless candles throwing light over the manor. Giggling like children, they hurried down the corridor to the darkened library. Henry twisted the lock closed behind them. Candle in hand, he faced Adelle.

"We only have a few minutes," he warned her. "We're the hosts. Someone will come looking for us eventually."

She looped her arms around his neck. "We'll just have to make the most of this, won't we?"

He pushed a few books off the top of a nearby table and lifted her onto it. He pushed up the skirts of her dark green gown, hands caressing the tops of her thighs over her stockings. His kiss was fierce and demanding, his tongue teasing her lips apart.

"I didn't know stealing away like this had this effect on you," she gasped. His teeth nipped at her neck, something he always did, but she enjoyed it.

"Neither did I." She heard the smile in his voice.

With fumbling hands, she helped him unbutton his trousers and free himself. Without any more words, he pushed inside her, a move that pulled the air from her lungs.

"Did I hurt you?" he asked.

"Of course not." She heard voices from somewhere in the corridor, and from the way he paused, he must have, too. She felt full, but it wasn't enough. "Henry, we don't have much time. I need you."

That was all the urging he needed. She gripped the edge of the table to keep from sliding off as he thrust into her, her hips meeting his, his ragged breaths filling her ears. The motion set off her climax, her cry muffled with his mouth over hers.

Still tingling with aftershocks, his tempo increased, and

she knew he was close, too. With a groan he couldn't muffle, he pulled out of her body, hands scrabbling in his pocket for a handkerchief.

Neither of them spoke for a moment. Henry leaned his forehead against hers. "I almost didn't make it," he whispered, and Adelle knew what he was referring to.

Some of her euphoria evaporated. "Would it be so awful if we had a baby?"

A pained look briefly crossed his face. Was he really so afraid of having children? It was bound to happen sooner or later. Adelle slid off the table and adjusted her skirts. "Please don't be frightened," she whispered. "I love you."

Relief crossed his face, but when he spoke, she could hear the pain in his voice. "Oh, Adelle, I love you, too."

A thrill soared through her, and tears sprang to her eyes.

He wrapped his arms around her and kissed her forehead. "Whatever happens between us, please don't ever doubt that."

His ominous words had all the effect on her as being doused with a bucket of cold water, and once again, she wondered what he was hiding. Uneasiness pulled her as possessively as his fingers gripped hers as he led her from the library.

In the time they were away, the guests' spirits appeared to have risen further, and no one asked where she and Henry had disappeared to. Adelle caught sight of herself in a looking glass and was relieved to see that aside from higher color in her cheeks and a dark curl worked loose from its hairpins, she looked as she did at the beginning of the evening. Still, she smoothed her hair and watched as Henry did the same.

Now she indulged in a glass of wine and surveyed her handiwork, trying to put Henry's statement behind her.

She enjoyed running her own household, more than she expected, and she was pleased to see she could successfully host a ball. *I'll do this again,* she told herself. Possibly in the summer. She would have to ask Henry when the best time would be.

She spotted him on the other side of the ballroom, speaking with a group of farmers. He caught her eye and smiled.

She returned it and was still smiling when the ballroom doors burst open with a resounding crack, and a black-clad Duke of Wexfield strode inside.

CHAPTER 7

Screams rang throughout the ballroom, echoing off its walls. But Adelle remained silent and frozen in place, staring at Wexfield in shock, her wineglass gripped so tightly in her hand Henry thought it might shatter.

It was the sight of his terrified wife that had him springing into action and crossing the room with an uncanny speed. Rage colored his vision, the urge to shift into his wolf form nearly overwhelming. A rational part of him knew he would shift before the night was over, as well as the other wolves present who could change without a full moon.

Three. There are three other wolves here tonight who can shift of their own will.

As far as he knew, all of them could control their shifting when under stress, but tonight was not the time to find that out for sure. Nothing like this had ever happened to the barony before.

It wasn't just that Wexfield invaded his home, although that was maddening. He must have forced his way in through the foyer doors, and he wouldn't have noticed it when he was in the library with Adelle.

It was the threats to his wife that galled Henry the most, closely followed by those against his pack. He could live without the manor or title, if he truly had to, as long as he could take care of the pack. Hell, he didn't feel like a member of the aristocracy, anyway, nor did he live like the typical one. But he'd found a kind of peace and happiness that he never expected to find with Adelle, and giving those up was no longer possible.

"What do you want?" Henry's shout bounced off the walls, and a few people shrank even farther away. "What is the meaning of this?"

"MacAulay, we both know what you are," Wexfield boomed. He pushed aside his black coat enough to reveal the pistol holstered at his hip, and Henry pushed Adelle behind him. He'd never been shot, but he knew he had a better chance of surviving such a wound than Adelle.

A cold knot of dread joined the fury bubbling up in him.

You should have told her weeks ago, fool!

He could hear and feel every shallow, panicked breath she took, and he desperately wished he could make this intruder disappear.

"I passed some time in the royal libraries these last weeks, MacAulay," Wexfield said. "It seems there's a fantastic story surrounding the first Baron of Roseheath and how an inhospitable, godforsaken tract of land and its wretched inhabitants came to be totally cut off from the rest of Britain, and a shape-shifting abomination made his way into the gentry."

If Wexfield knew, he had to die. There was no other way around it.

Henry pushed aside his guilt and looked Wexfield in

his good eye. The Duke didn't cower or look down, a show of insubordination that only further agitated his wolf.

"If you know the story," Henry said, "then you know I and my wolves are sanctioned to kill you."

"Wolves?" Adelle whispered.

Wexfield heard her, too, as did the entire ballroom. For a few seconds, it was silent as to hear a pin drop.

Then the duke let out a hearty laugh, a noise that sounded forced. "MacAulay, your wife doesn't know?" he asked.

"Know what?" Adelle said. "Henry, what is he talking about?"

"Adelle," he said urgently, but Wexfield cut him off.

"My lady," Wexfield said in an exaggerated voice. He was enjoying this, the bastard. "You're married to an abomination. Your husband is a werewolf."

She sucked in a harsh breath. "You're out of your mind," she said, but she didn't sound sure of herself. Henry could see she was piecing together every strange thing that had happened in the barony since her arrival: the secrets, the wolves themselves, the staff's deference to him in the days leading up to the full moon. Possibly even his being so territorial about having guests in his home. Pain and regret speared him, but he couldn't do anything about that now.

And it was all his fault.

Henry heard a low growl behind him, but didn't dare turn around. He recognized the man behind it—Speller—and knew he was very quickly going to shift.

He forced himself to look Adelle in the eye. Her expression was a mix of confusion and terror. She darted a quick glance at Speller, whose face was already beginning to sprout fur. "What is he talking about?" she asked again.

An edge of panic crept into her voice. "What's happening?"

He pressed a quick kiss to her lips, praying it wouldn't be the last time he did. "I'm sorry," he said simply.

Turning to Wexfield, he asked, "Why are you here?" He let his alpha wolf's personality surface, tossing aside everything remotely genteel about him. He closed the short distance between him and the duke until they were nearly nose-to-nose.

He didn't smell a trace of fear on the man, and that only served to make him angrier. "I have a problem, MacAulay," Wexfield said. "You're the only animal I know who can help me."

A growl rose in Henry's throat. A few of his fellow wolves moved closer to Wexfield, ready to tear him to pieces on the orders of their alpha.

"Nobody move!" Henry's voice was sharp, and everyone assembled knew to obey him. Wexfield was armed. Henry could smell the gunpowder and knew the weapon was loaded. Everyone was still in their human form, and no one had any weapons.

He kept his gaze trained on Wexfield's, willing the man to cower. He didn't. "There's only one animal here," Henry said. "And none of them are from my pack."

"There's no need for that," Wexfield said. "I'm dying, MacAulay. I need your help."

"You're a dead man anyway," Henry promised him.

A bitter smile twisted Wexfield's face. "No. I have a disease in my lungs. My physicians tell me it's a matter of months. I'll be dead before Christmas."

"I fail to see why that's my problem."

"It's your problem because if you don't change me into one of you, I'll simply kill Adelle." He touched the gun at his hip and more growls sounded through the ballroom, but Henry held up his hand to keep anyone from attacking him. While he couldn't smell fear on Wexfield, he could feel the desperation clinging to the man, and he knew what he said of a disease in his lungs was true. The man didn't want to die, but he didn't have any compunction about killing Adelle to ensure it didn't happen.

Even though what the duke wanted wasn't possible.

Henry felt his gums itch and his teeth lengthen, desperate to rip out of the man's throat. He forced back the change and remained unmoving. "No."

"No, you want me to kill your wife instead?"

"No, I cannot change you. That isn't how werewolves are made."

"What in God's name?" Adelle whispered. In Henry's singular focus on the duke, she sounded far away, and both incredulous and terrified.

Wexfield shook his head. "I don't believe you."

"It's true," Henry said. "Wolves aren't made."

"The stories at the library spoke of changing dying men," Wexfield insisted. "I read them. It's possible, and someone here is going to do it tonight."

Henry shook his head. "If they do, then they're wrong. If we could change regular men into wolves, our pack would have done that decades ago. We're a small group and getting smaller." He hoped his voice didn't betray him when he continued. "It's one of the reasons I didn't fight when Adelle was sent to me. We need new blood, and soon."

Adelle's hurt cry tore at his heart, but he didn't turn around to apologize. It was the truth, and she deserved to know long ago. Not here or now, and he again he cursed himself for delaying telling her.

The sound of clothing shredding followed by a wet snarl had Wexfield looking over Henry's shoulder. When

Henry looked behind him, he saw Speller making a brutal change, fur sprouting over his face and hands, limbs lengthening. Bone and muscle made slick, popping noises as it was rearranged, and a thump reverberated on the polished floor when Speller fell on four massive paws.

Adelle stared at him, horror and disgust evident on her features, the odor of fright heavy in the air. Her mouth opened as if to scream, but nothing came out. She turned panicked eyes to Henry's face, and he saw realization dawn in them.

She knew what he was. She believed her eyes at everything that was happening before her.

Spurred by the sight of their friend, a few of the other wolves began to change, too. Wolves that had never changed before outside of a full moon. Henry cursed at them in his mind; it would only make things worse.

He fought against the urge to shift, knowing his rage and the surrounding wolves were going to make that even more difficult. "They will kill you," he warned Wexfield.

They wouldn't. As soon as the duke turned around, Henry would kill him himself. Wexfield could not go back to London with stories about werewolves.

A faint trace of the duke's fear finally drifted to Henry's nostrils. He allowed himself a tiny smile. At last, it appeared that Wexfield understood what was happening, just what he had set in motion.

The moment quickly passed, and smug arrogance again crossed Wexfield's features. He tore the pistol from the holster under his coat and closed the short distance between them, reaching behind Henry to snatch Adelle's arm. He pulled her away, holding his gun at her temple.

"Are any of you willing to risk her life or yours?" he said.

The ballroom remained silent save for a few growls

near the back. More shifting would occur soon. Henry was close to it, too.

"The duke means what he says," Henry said. Speller nudged his snout at Henry's thigh, which he ignored. He would not be prodded into an impulsive, foolish action right now. He had to remain calm as long as possible, keep his wolf from springing out and further endangering Adelle, and take care of Wexfield.

Three things. You can do them.

"Leave my wife and pack alone," Henry said. "We will discuss this rationally."

More sounds of ripping clothes throughout the ball-room meant that the time for rationality had passed.

Wexfield's hand dug into Adelle's waist, and his grip on the weapon tightened. Adelle squeezed her eyes shut, tears sliding down her face. "Like men?" he mocked.

Henry forced back a growl. "Like the wolf man you wish to be."

"Not here," Wexfield demanded, his good eye taking in the werewolves shifting around him.

"The library, then." Before he led the duke out of the ballroom, he added, "If you so much as harm a hair on her head, I will kill you."

"How so? You've forgotten, MacAulay, that I have the gun and silver bullets."

The bullets wouldn't do any more harm than regular ones, but Henry wouldn't let Wexfield know that. "I'm an alpha wolf," he said simply. "I have the most control over my emotions and my shifting. I can change far faster than the others in my pack, and I don't need a full moon to do it, either. Some wolves have that problem."

Wexfield merely looked irritated at his explanation. "To your library."

"Let go of Adelle, or I won't talk to you." Henry wasn't

going to talk, anyway. As soon as he got the man out of the ballroom, he was going to kill him.

Wexfield hesitated for a few seconds, but he relinquished his hold on Adelle and pushed her into Henry. She immediately backed away from him, stark fear in her eyes. They drifted down to the massive wolf pacing behind Henry and widened.

"Adelle," he whispered. "I'm so sorry. I should have told you, I wanted to tell you…"

She shook her head. "No," she whispered.

No. What did she mean by that? He didn't have time to think about it.

"Speller," Henry said, his voice carrying through the ballroom. The wolf sat on his haunches and looked up at him. "Miller, Fitzgerald. You three will accompany me to the library." Before Wexfield could protest, he added, "I don't trust you, and if you want to be a wolf, you will learn to submit to my authority. Your title has no meaning in Roseheath. *I'm* the only alpha wolf in this pack."

Miller and Fitzgerald, the other wolves who could easily shift outside of a full moon, hadn't yet changed, but Henry could tell from their enlarged pupils they weren't far off from it. At least they had kept some control, unlike the others who spontaneously changed. "Leave the ballroom and turn left," he ordered Wexfield. "I don't trust you not to shoot me in the back."

Wexfield held up his hands in a mockery of surrender. That damned clockwork eye whirred, the tinny noise making Henry want to rip it out of his face. "Very well."

He was plotting something, but Henry couldn't sense what it was.

"I'm going with you," Adelle said, finally finding her voice.

"No," Henry snapped. "Absolutely not."

She hissed in his ear, "You're hardly in a position to be telling me what to do."

"I am. This isn't safe."

"You *bastard*," she whispered harshly. He heard the agony in her voice and hated himself for it. "You may be the alpha of this *pack*, but you are *not* mine." She enunciated her next words carefully. "I am. Going with you. To the *library*."

Henry didn't argue with her. Instead, he walked out of the ballroom, flanked by his wolves. Adelle followed them, but he didn't acknowledge her.

Once in the corridor, he continued barking out instructions until they reached the library. He recalled with pain what had happened in here so shortly before with Adelle, and a quick glance at her mortified face told him she was thinking the same thing.

Wexfield sprawled in a chair as if it belonged to him. "How does one go about changing?" he asked casually.

"How exactly are you ill?"

"A disease of the lungs, as I told you. My physician believes I may have picked it up when I was still investing in the mining business. A common thing," he said disdainfully. "I've been searching for treatments these last few months since I found out it's incurable." He coughed, the sound wet and phlegmy. Away from the ballroom and its smells of food and the tenants, he could now smell the cough remedy on the duke, a faint but no less revolting stench of something medicinal Henry couldn't quite identify, overlaid with mint.

"And that's how you found out about our pack?" Miller asked. A short look from Henry shut him up. He and Wexfield would be the only ones speaking.

"No, I came across that story when I was looking for information about the barony after Adelle rejected my proposal. The Thornber family is quite wealthy, you know," he said, nodding in Adelle's direction. "Adelle's dowry would have been helpful in paying for treatment. They're doing incredible things across the Channel. I needed a rich wife and heirs far more than *you* ever did. I will not stand for my bastard of a nephew to inherit my title." He smiled, but it rang false. "It turns out that changing into one of you is better than marrying a disgraced heiress."

Before Henry could reply to this, Adelle laughed, a harsh sound devoid of mirth. "Wexfield, I barely had a dowry. My family is nearly bankrupt, thanks to my father's gambling habits."

Wexfield stared at her, disbelief plain on his face. "No."

"Why do you think they were so willing to be rid of me? It wasn't just because of my affair with Will," she said. "I was another mouth to feed, and I hadn't found a husband on my own. Of course they wanted me out of the house," she said. "And how is it that you of all people can't pay for your treatment?"

"It's running me dry," he admitted. "And I made some a poor investment that wouldn't have been so devastating if I wasn't ill. I can either die, or I can change into a wolfman. They don't acquire these diseases."

That wasn't true, but Henry didn't point it out. Werewolves were certainly hardier than humans, but they weren't infallible.

Wexfield's expression hardened. "Change me."

Henry looked at Adelle. "Leave," he ordered. He did not want her to see him kill the duke. He didn't want her to hate him more than she already did.

She held firm. "No."

"You won't want to see this."

"I've seen a lot tonight that I never expected to," she said acidly.

"Oh, fuck off," Wexfield snapped. Drawing his weapon again, he aimed it at Adelle. "If you have to leave for him to change me, leave the room. For once in your pathetic life, don't act like a simpering whore."

The insult was the final undoing to Henry's control. His shift to wolf form was swift and brutal, the sounds of his evening clothes ripping too loudly for his heightened senses, as was Adelle's shriek. Miller and Fitzgerald quickly followed their alpha's lead until four huge wolves circled him.

"Is this it, then?" Wexfield asked. "You're going to attack me instead?"

He was smarter than Henry gave him credit for. He crouched on his hind legs to lunge at him, but the sharp crack of Wexfield's gun firing made him pause.

Adelle screamed again, and Speller jumped. Miller whined and slumped to the ground. He shook his hind leg, blood blooming across his light fur.

Henry pounced, knocking Wexfield to the carpeted floor. Jaws snapping, he tried to reach for the man's throat, but the duke fought back. He was stronger than Henry expected, but human stamina wasn't that of a werewolf's, especially when he was ill. Wexfield would wear out soon enough.

The gun fired again, the sound so loud it had Henry's ears ringing. When they stopped, he realized Adelle was screaming in pain. When he whipped his head around, he saw her fall back against the library door, blood rushing from between the fingers she held against a wound in her side. Rage colored Henry's vision at the sight.

Shock seemed to have temporarily blindsided the duke as he stared at Adelle, because for the first time since he barged into the ballroom, he was frozen in place. Henry leaped back on to Wexfield, his jaws clenching around the muscle joining his neck and shoulder.

There was another loud bang, and a searing pain ripped into Henry's abdomen. He didn't let go of Wexfield until he felt himself grow drowsy, his eyes too heavy to keep open.

CHAPTER 8

e had been sleeping for nearly three days.

Adelle spent the time watching over Henry, trying to decide whether she should stay, return to London, or collect her dowry from him and start life over overseas. None of those options looked especially bright. Henry had lied to her during their entire marriage, she would be asked questions about Wexfield in London as well as having to deal with her family again, and she knew she was even more ill-prepared to live in another country than she had been in a ramshackle manor in Scotland.

So she stayed at Henry's bedside, occasionally leaving to eat and inspect her own healing wound.

Roseheath's physician had taken the room across the corridor from Henry's old bedroom, spending the first evening and the day after caring for him. Her husband had changed back into a human shortly after he was shot, after he had finally been pulled away from the flailing, screaming Wexfield by guests who heard the gunshots. The process of changing back seemed to be even more grue-some than his shifting into wolf form.

The coppery smell of blood still filled Adelle's nose when she tried to sleep. She sat up beside Henry's bed instead, thinking about what she could do about this situation.

Henry owed her an explanation. She wouldn't leave until she received it.

On the morning of the third day after the ball, he stirred and opened his eyes. Surprise lit them up, and he immediately tried to sit. "You're still here," he said.

She rose from her seat and pushed on his bare shoulders until he rested back against the pillows. "I am," she said curtly. "Let me get Dr. Haver." Before he could protest, she quickly left the room to fetch the doctor.

She stayed in the corridor while the physician fussed over Henry, letting Mrs. Tuplin give her tea. The housekeeper had been very quiet since the night of the ball, not offering any unsolicited advice or opinions. Everyone in the barony had avoided Adelle except to ask quick questions about Henry, likely unsure of how the lady of the manor would react once her werewolf husband woke up.

Adelle didn't know how she would react, either.

She returned to Henry's bedroom an hour later. He was still awake and managed to haul himself up to a sitting position, his hand pressed against his bandaged abdomen. His eyes were dark and sad when he looked at Adelle. "You haven't left," he said softly, as if he couldn't believe she was before him.

She shook her head, willing her tears away. She hated crying when she was angry, hated displaying that kind of weakness.

"How badly were you hurt?" he asked.

"Wexfield's bullet grazed me on my side. It looked much worse than it actually was." The bullet ended up lodged in the wall behind her. "I'm already on the mend.

Your friend Mr. Miller will be all right, too." The werewolf had a bullet removed from his leg but was already healing.

"I'm glad to hear that." They were silent for a moment, staring at each other in a quiet battle of wills.

Henry finally spoke. "Adelle, there is nothing I can say that would erase what I've done to you," he said. "I'm sorry, and I know that's not enough."

She wiped away a tear. "No, it's not." She took her seat beside the bed, waiting for him to continue.

"I wanted to tell you," he said. "I tried. But I couldn't do it. It's why I couldn't bring myself to mark you as my mate, because you needed to know first." He looked at the ceiling, collecting his thoughts. "What an alpha wolf I make, don't I?"

"I wouldn't know," she said bitterly. "I know almost nothing about werewolves except that they exist. That was you outside my window that night, wasn't it?"

He nodded.

"It's all werewolves here, isn't it?" she asked. "Were you going to make me one of them?"

"As I told Wexfield, that isn't possible."

She swallowed past the lump in her throat. "Were you ever going to tell me about our children being wolves?"

"Yes. I meant to tell you everything," he said. "I didn't know how. You're the first outsider to come to Roseheath in decades, and…" His voice broke, and he looked away. "You weren't what I was expecting."

Adelle kept her eyes on the fire crackling in the hearth.

"I fell in love with you," Henry said. "I hope you believe that. I think it could have been easier, in a way, if I hadn't, because it wouldn't matter as much if you thought me a monster."

"I saw you rip into Wexfield's neck!" Adelle had

loathed the man, but that didn't take away from her shock at seeing her husband attack him.

"He wanted to kill you. That's why I didn't want you to come to the library." He sighed in dismay. "Dr. Haver told me what happened to him."

Wexfield succumbed to his wounds shortly after Henry collapsed. His last words were hissed to Adelle: "You bitch."

Standing up again, she paced around the bed. "Tell me this. If I leave, will you or one of the other wolves kill me to keep me from speaking about this in London?"

"No!" he insisted, clearly horrified. "I don't ever want you to stay here if you don't want to. Adelle, I know how selfish it was for me not to have told you about this. But I would never keep you from leaving."

The anguish on his face was genuine, and she knew he was telling the truth. But she still needed more questions answered.

"Why did Wexfield know about the wolves here?" she asked. "Is this something everything knows except me? How long has this been going on?" The anger that had been simmering since they were shot now bubbled to the surface.

Henry took a deep breath and told her about his family history: the werewolf pack's deal with England, and the generations of peace that had come about because of it. "I may have to contact the queen and ask her to remove those medieval records from her library," he said. "I don't want to risk someone else getting ideas about coming here."

"Why would there be records in the first place?" she asked.

"They're stories," he explained. "Things of legend. It's true that our pack was at war with humans hundreds of years ago, and someone wrote it down and forgot about it.

No one would believe stories about werewolves, anyway, and of course, we've taken care not to correct any misconceptions others may have about us. Silver doesn't affect us, for instance."

"Except Wexfield believed those stories."

"Except him," he said. "He was a desperate man. Either for you and your family's fortune or a cure. But as fantastic as those werewolf stories are, those records have to go." He winced and touched his bandaged side.

"And Roseheath has been left alone all these years?"

"The first baron and the king he struck the deal with agreed to stay away from each other, and we've all done that through the years. No one goes farther than Edinburgh, and no one comes here."

"Except me."

He nodded. "Our arranged marriage was the only demand ever placed on Roseheath, and as I told you about the threats to my patents, that's why I didn't fight it."

Adelle shook her head, absorbing this information. She didn't know how she should feel after these revelations, and her heart, the irrational thing it was, still ached for him.

She still loved him. She didn't think she could ever stop.

"What about Mrs. Tuplin?" she asked. "Or Bensfort? Is this whole village full of werewolves?"

He shook his head. "They're descended from werewolves, and Mrs. Tuplin's son and daughter are. Not everyone in the barony is a wolf, but everyone is related to one and knows about them."

"Everyone in your immediate family is a wolf," she said. She remembered the portraits of some long-dead barons, standing next to wolves. Themselves in their other forms, she knew now.

"Everyone in my family is, yes," he said. "Although I'm

the only one at the moment. MacAulay children are always wolves."

"That explains why you've been so careful," she muttered.

"Because I wanted to tell you first," he said.

Her voice rose. "And what do you think I would have done?"

"I don't know!" He gave a frustrated sigh. 'Would you have believed me?"

That was a question Adelle had been contemplating since the ball, and she didn't know the answer. "I don't know," she said, echoing his words.

"It wasn't just my being a wolf," Henry said. "I wanted you all to myself for a while. I wanted us to get to know one another before we started a family."

"God damn it," she muttered. Surprise crossed Henry's face when she uttered the epithet, but he didn't comment on it. "Do you know how frustrating it is when you love someone and something like this happens?"

"No."

"It was terrifying to see you shift," she said. "I still can't get past that. It looked painful to experience, and I…" Her voice cracked. "I didn't believe what I was seeing at first. I couldn't believe it was still you as a wolf."

"What if I shifted for you?" His hand reached for hers, stroking her knuckles with calloused fingertips. And God help her, that small motion felt good. "You'll see it's still me. Just in a different form."

She considered what he was saying and realized she needed to see him do that when she wasn't scared for their lives. "All right." She sat down heavily on the bed next to him, noting the hopeful look on his face.

"I can shift now, if you want," he said. "I don't need a full moon to do it. Most of the other wolves do. I'm not sure what happened during your party." He winced and touched the bandages wrapped around his abdomen. "I'm so sorry I spoiled your party."

"I'm not sure doing that now a good idea," she said. "You have stitches. And you didn't spoil my party. You had help."

"I deserve that," he said. "And shifting can help the healing process along. Can you help me up?"

Adelle knew she wasn't going to win this argument. She pushed aside the bedsheets and let him lean on her as he hauled himself out of bed. Despite his bandages, she couldn't keep herself from being affected by his body, gloriously naked before her. A flush crept up her neck and she prayed he wouldn't notice.

No such luck. He offered her a rakish smile, as if he could read her mind. He pulled at the bandages, stripping them off and tossing them on the fire. The wound on his stomach was an angry miasma of red and purple, crisscrossed with black sutures.

"Are you sure that's wise?" Adelle asked.

"I don't know. I'll likely feel better after I shift, though."

"You've done this before?" Despite her anger, she felt their old camaraderie returning.

"I've never been shot before," he admitted. "But I broke a leg when I was a boy and shifting helped with the healing." He took a few steps closer to her, and she didn't move away. "May I kiss you before I do this?"

She nodded.

It was a hungry kiss that left her weak in the knees and was over far too soon. She doubted he would ever stop having that effect on her.

Something he said earlier came to mind. "What did you mean when you said you wanted to mark me?" she asked.

He rolled one of his shoulders, his skin glowing in the firelight. "Wolves sometimes mark their mates," he said. "Just a small bite on their necks, usually."

"And I'm your mate? How does that work?"

"It's something wolves do as a sort of claiming," he explained. "It's instinctual, and I never believed in it until I met you." He flushed, which Adelle thought adorable. "It's, uh, a primal, territorial. So other wolves will know you've been claimed."

His words warmed her, and not just physically. "How do you do that?" He looked back at the bed, and she felt herself blush. "*Oh.*"

"It isn't strictly necessary, but it helps," he said.

Now she felt that physically.

Henry took a few steps back from her and closed his eyes, breathing deeply. A growl rose in his throat, and dark fur sprouted from his hands, arms, face—everywhere. His face changed shape, his nose lengthening into a snout, and fangs appeared where his teeth should be. Flesh stretched with a wet noise over expanding bone and muscle until he fell to the floor on huge paws. He was the largest animal she had ever seen.

The massive wolf nudged Adelle's hand with his nose, and not knowing what to do, she patted his head. He turned dark, familiar eyes up to her, and any trepidation she felt evaporated.

This was Henry, and she still loved him. It would take some time to get used to being married to a werewolf, but he was still the same man she met outside the manor on that cold night so many weeks ago.

She ran her hands down his back, his shaggy fur thick and a little prickly. She couldn't tell if his wound had opened up again, and he didn't give any indication that it was bothering him.

How did one address a werewolf? "Hello again," she said. She tentatively scratched his ear, and he tilted his head to the side, clearly enjoying it.

When she stopped, he sniffed at her skirts, then padded to the door. He scratched at it with a paw. Adelle opened it, and he stuck his head into the corridor, tail swishing.

There was a shriek, followed by Mrs. Tuplin's wail. "Not inside the house! I never let my husband shift in the house, and you won't either!" There was a pause, and then she called, "My lady? Are you all right?"

"I'm fine," Adelle said, stepping into the corridor. She placed a hand on his furry back. "Henry told me everything."

"Should have done that a long time ago," the housekeeper said with a sniff.

"You're right." Adelle shot a pointed look at Henry, who lowered his head and backed into the room. "He should have."

She followed him back in and closed the door behind them. Henry grunted, and the shifting sounds again filled the room.

A few moments later, her husband was human again, hunched over the bedclothes and breathing heavily. He flopped on his back, and Adelle saw that his sutures had popped out during the transformation. His wound looked better though, weeks old instead of only three days.

"How is it?" she asked, gesturing at his stomach.

"A little sore, but much better. I'm healing. I don't know if I'll want to shift during the next full moon." He sat upright and smiled, making Adelle's heart turn over. He was still naked, and it was very much a distraction.

"Do you have to shift?"

"We're compelled to do it," he explained. "Although I suspect now that extreme stress can cause it, as you saw in the ballroom. I've never seen that happen in my pack before. It does feel good to be among your own kind, working together for a common goal. Even if that goal is to eliminate a threat to your way of life."

She tried and failed to tamp down her hurt. "I see."

She wasn't one of his kind, and he had made it clear being so wouldn't be possible.

His expression softened. "Adelle, come here."

She sat down on the bed next to him. "It isn't just the other wolves now," he said softly, breath stirring her hair. "It's you, too."

"I'm 'one of your kind', then?"

His reply was swift. "Yes. You're the most important person in my life. I love you very much, Adelle, and I hope you'll forgive me someday."

His words tugged at her, and she wrapped her arms around him. "It will take a while to forget, but I'll forgive you," she said. "There's just one more thing I have to ask, and you have to answer it honestly."

"Anything."

"Are there any other secrets?"

"No," he said. "None. Unless you count the flameless candle. I'm ready to file a patent. I haven't told anyone yet."

"That's it? Only the candles?"

"*Only* the candles? I've been working on them for years," he teased. He immediately sobered. "Yes, that's it."

"All right."

Once again, she was very aware that he was undressed, and she wasn't. She leaned around him and half-pulled a sheet over him. "This is distracting."

"So you want me to dress?" he asked.

"It's not really fair that you get to distract me like this."

"I could either dress, or you could undress."

Adelle considered this for a half-second before reaching for her blouse's buttons. "I need help," she said.

He helped her with the buttons. "I mean it, you know," he said, peeling the dress off her shoulders. "I love you so much."

She touched his cheek. He leaned into her hand and kissed her palm. "I love you, too, Henry."

Henry helped her push the garment to the floor, unknotting her corset strings next. "Is the door locked?"

She looked at it. "I don't know. Possibly."

"Can I mark you?"

She turned startled eyes to him. It sounded like such a primitive thing to do, but the idea of it felt exciting.

He mistook her surprise for hesitation. "If you don't want me to, I won't."

"Will it hurt?"

"I don't know. I've never marked anyone before."

She pressed her forehead against his. "Do it."

His lips eagerly met hers, his tongue sweeping into her mouth. He rudely pushed aside her corset; his fingers scrabbled against her stockings, tearing the silk. His arousal pressed against her hip, hot and insistent. It wasn't enough.

His mouth moved over her neck, where her pulse beat in a rapid tattoo. He bit down on the soft flesh there, breaking the skin a little and pulling a startled gasp from her. Just as quickly, he ran his tongue over it, erasing the hurt as if it never happened. He propped himself up on his elbows.

"You're mine," he said.

They were words Adelle had never thought to hear. That should have been terrifying, but from him, they made her feel loved and wanted. She touched the spot on her neck, felt the raised mark there, and knew it would be permanent. She quickly angled her head over Henry's neck and bit him in the same spot.

"You're mine, too," she said smugly.

Instead of laughing off her attempt to mark him, he simply laced his fingers through hers in a romantic gesture. His eyes met hers and held on. "I always was."

AUTHOR'S NOTE

Wolf's Lady was the first book I sold to a publisher.

Pulling it apart and sewing it back together when its rights reverted was a bright spot for me in the unprecedented fuckery that was 2020. I'm happy to have given it a makeover: I've expanded it a little, and consent between Adelle and Henry is clearer in the new edition than it was previously.

Some of you may note that besides the lack of flight travel and availability of steam-powered prosthetics in 1887, barons weren't and continue to not be a thing in Scotland as Henry is written. Neither are wolves for that matter, anywhere in Britain. But if you've made it this far, you're not reading *Wolf's Lady* for its historical accuracy.

Thank you for reading!

Jess Marting

ABOUT THE AUTHOR

Jessica Marting is a sci-fi and paranormal romance author, art enthusiast (not quite an artist, despite all that time in art school), an avid reader, and makeup collector. She lives in Toronto.

Newsletter:
  http://jessicamarting.com/newsletter